A copywriter, Lynette Clarke has carved a career working with words. *The Rat Cage* is her third book but first fictional novel. When she is not writing, she lectures at universities in Australia and Singapore.

For my son, Sam, with love.

In memory of my parents, William and Sylvia Clarke, forever in my heart.

Lynette Clarke

The Rat Cage

Austin Macauley Publishers™
London * Cambridge * New York * Sharjah

This is a work of fiction. Names, characters, businesses, places, events, locales, and incidents are either the products of the author's imagination or used in a fictitious manner. Any resemblance to actual persons, living or dead, or actual events is purely coincidental.

A CIP catalogue record for this title is available from the British Library.

ISBN 9781035801404 (Paperback)
ISBN 9781035801411 (Hardback)
ISBN 9781035801428 (ePub e-book)

www.austinmacauley.com

First Published 2024
Austin Macauley Publishers Ltd®
1 Canada Square
Canary Wharf
London
E14 5AA

20240405

Cover design by Benny Moore (*bennymooredesign.com*). Thank you Benny. Your ability to convey so much so simply never ceases to amaze me.

While this is a work of fiction, I am so grateful for the plethora of background information provided by numerous documents, articles, posts and blogs. In fact, the wonderful experiences, stories and findings that I came across have actually turned a phobia into a new-found respect.

https://journals.openedition.org/osb/1765
https://www.unodc.org/documents/scientific/ST_NAR_26_E.pdf
https://en.wikipedia.org/wiki/Laboratory_rat
https://en.wikipedia.org/wiki/Black_rat
https://www.britannica.com/summary/rat
https://www.sciencedirect.com/science/article/abs/pii/S009167737790308X
https://www.parsemus.org/wp-content/uploads/2019/08/Calcium-chloride-chemical-castration-in-the-rat.pdf
http://www.horns.freeserve.co.uk/ratneuter.htm
https://www.ncbi.nlm.nih.gov/pmc/articles/PMC2750945/
https://www.sciencedirect.com/science/article/abs/pii/0022473188903093
https://pubmed.ncbi.nlm.nih.gov/14727892/
https://pubmed.ncbi.nlm.nih.gov/2201007/
https://api.parliament.uk/historichansard/commons/1984/jun/12/london-economic-summit
https://api.parliament.uk/historic-hansard/people/mrs-margaret-thatcher/1984
https://www.ncbi.nlm.nih.gov/pmc/articles/PMC6738345/
https://psycnet.apa.org/record/1949-02128-001
http://www.horns.freeserve.co.uk/introrats3.htm
https://www.hsccvt.org/files/galleries/Rat_Information.pdf
https://en.wikipedia.org/wiki/Battle_of_Orgreave
https://www.bbc.com/news/uk-37562740

https://medium.com/read-about-it/remembering-the-battle-of-orgreave-4ae597d84020
https://www.smithsonianmag.com/science-nature/archaeological-treasures-hidden-rat-nests-180973544/
https://animals.mom.com/signs-female-rat-pregnant-1865.html
https://www.ratforum.com/threads/phantom-pregnancy-or-are-they-pregnant.28577/
https://www.ratshackforum.com/threads/hormones-phantom-pregnancy-ocd-behaviours.14372/
http://www.ratbehavior.org/Hybridization.htm
https://ratguide.com/care/environment/cage_bedding_litter.php
https://sssb.se/en/wp-content/uploads/sites/2/Facts_ratsmice_ENG.pdf
http://www.isamurats.co.uk/rats-fighting-aggression-and-dominant-behaviour.html
https://journals.sagepub.com/doi/10.1177/0023677215618618
https://www.animalwised.com/what-do-rats-eat-in-the-wild-rat-diet-3232.html
https://www.ncbi.nlm.nih.gov/pmc/articles/PMC4585313/
https://www.livescience.com/52342-rats.html

Table of Contents

The Beginning of the End **11**

Chapter 1 **12**

10 June 1984 *18*

Chapter 2 **19**

17 June 1984 *24*

Chapter 3 **26**

24 June 1984 *33*

Chapter 4 **34**

28 June 1984 *39*

Chapter 5 **40**

Chapter 6 **44**

8 July 1984 *50*

Chapter 7 **51**

15 July 1984 *57*

Chapter 8 **59**

22 July 1984 *65*

Chapter 9 **66**

29 July 1984 *70*

Chapter 10 **71**

5 August 1984 *78*

Chapter 11 **79**

12 August 1984 *84*

Chapter 12 **85**

19 August 1984 *92*

Chapter 13 **94**

26 August 1984 *100*

Chapter 14 **101**

2 September 1984 *110*

Chapter 15 **111**

Chapter 16 **122**

9 September 1984 *129*

Chapter 17 **130**

16 September 1984 *141*

Chapter 18 **142**

20 September 1984 *150*

Chapter 19 **151**

Chapter 20 **159**

25 September 1984 *171*

Chapter 21 **172**

30 September 1984 *181*

Chapter 22 **182**

Obituary **194**

The Beginning of the End

It's weird what goes through your mind when you're about to die.

Those who've had near death experiences often speak of their lives flashing before their eyes. But no…so far…nothing.

I also didn't expect to be dying with someone else, yet here I am with him and he's further along, not by much but enough, that I will see him pass before I take my last breath.

I had thought, from time to time, of how I might die but this never made my list. Maybe I could still have that stroke. I can only hope.

Am I scared? I can't think about that now. My head is hazy but I'm trying to keep my wits. You see, when your breaths are fast approaching single numbers, there's only one thing you want to know. It's something we've never been able to answer all the time we've been alive. Some of us never get the chance to work it out. But here I am and if I think clearly, I can get it, know it, put the last piece of my interlude on this Earth in place.

Then suddenly, probably because I had briefly been thinking of other things, it comes to me.

Sunday, September 30, 1984. That is the date of my death.

Chapter 1

The door burst open and they were there, the couple ones, standing in my space and yelling. I was now in the middle of an argument about someone, guessing it was him, going through her things. Throwing her bag onto the bunk, it toppled off the side and crashed at my feet. Bending down I retrieved a tube of lipstick and a hairbrush. She snatched them from my hand and tossed them back into her purse, seemingly now annoyed with me as well.

I share a room with five strangers. They are; the hairy one, the big girl, the student and this couple who were now arguing mainly in expletives, dotted here and there with an accusatory "always" or "never". Sensing I was in the way I managed to squeeze past them and, with nowhere else to go, headed downstairs.

I plonked myself into a large armchair near the entrance and glanced around. When I arrived, it was late at night but now, in the light of day, it was showing its age. Even the patterned carpet had been worn plain, except for the corners. There was a dankness in the air, despite it being summer. While hours after breakfast had been served, the smell of burnt toast and brewed tea lingered like so many of the residents.

A man sat opposite. Our eyes met and I smiled.

'Stop staring,' he snapped, 'and stop saying that. It's not true and you know it.'

I looked away and came face-to-face with another. He quickly jumped up and ran to the door.

I wondered if I should just return to my room. Going by their past outbursts, the couple guy would probably be gone now and, in the short time that I've been here, she and I have seemed to get along. Unlike the others who were always coming and going, she stayed in bed most days. In between naps, she teased her limp hair and applied lashings of eye make-up. During one of our chats, she told me she'd been an exotic dancer in Soho, fired for complaining that one of the stage props was dangerous. She now lived on welfare.

'Is this seat taken?'

I looked up to see a tanned face grinning at me.

'No, I don't think so,' I hesitated, wondering what had happened to the snappy man. But by then the tanned one had claimed the seat and was now tapping his fingers.

'I'm sorry,' he said, noticing me staring. 'Is that bothering you?'

'No, not really,' I lied, then regretted it immediately. The few words I'd said just to be polite had somehow been mistaken for a hand held out in friendship and he smiled widely, his white teeth fluorescent against his olive skin.

With no encouragement whatsoever, he was now divulging his life story. From his well-polished comedic-timing, including punchlines, I knew he'd performed this monologue before. He chatted about his time in the navy, the ports, the discipline, the freedom, even his stint in the Falkland Islands. He'd still be serving if his father hadn't died and he needed to care for his elderly mum. 'She's now passed away too,' he added, coughing to clear the sudden hoarseness in his throat. 'Been here for over 12 months would you believe?' I nodded and turned away, worried that I too would still be living here a year from now. 'So, what about you?' he asked, bringing me back to the present.

'Oh, I'm just visiting from Australia. Not much to tell.'

Suddenly his eyes opened wider as he leant in. I could tell by his body language that he believed the conversation was evolving into shared confidences, his mind busy compiling the questions he was going to ask.

'Hey, Tom, can you lend me your watch?'

The man who'd fled earlier had returned, and was now standing beside me with outstretched hand. I took this opportunity to leave.

Back in the room, she was alone, as I had suspected, and we became lost in our own thoughts. Doing nothing demands mental resolve and unlimited reserves of energy. I wondered whether I should sleep or eat. Neither option appealed.

'Do you lot ever go out?'

The silence was broken by the hairy one. Standing there with hands on hips, she eyed us both disapprovingly before locking herself in the bathroom. This girl was short with cropped dark curls, thick eyebrows and the hint of a moustache. For someone who appeared maintenance-free, she spent a great deal of time in the bathroom.

Now that her nail varnish was dry, the couple one popped some pills and, laying her head on the pillow, stared up at the ceiling. She was much quieter than her usual self.

'Are you okay?' I asked, not really caring, but feeling like I should enquire.

'Sure am, or will be, once these pills work.'

By the sound of her voice, she was almost asleep.

The manager at The Gazebo had told me to report on Tuesday at 10am. So, dressed in a white shirt, black skirt and comfortable shoes, I allowed myself plenty of time to walk the distance. Strolling through Kensington Gardens, things seemed to be picking up. However, my new-found optimism was short lived.

I swept and mopped floors, cleaned toilets, vacuumed carpets, polished glassware, set tables and all before the first patron arrived at midday. I had nine tables for both food and beverages. Not being familiar with the numbering system, I was reliant on my memory and it continually let me down.

'I didn't order the fish of the day.'

'We asked for garlic bread not herb.'

'Is that coffee coming?'

At closing, I realised I'd been on my feet for 12 hours.

The walk back was agony. My blistered heels kept rubbing against my new shoes and, in the end, I decided walking barefoot would be best. The only consolation was that I had seven pounds worth of tips.

Arriving in the room, I crashed on the bed, even the thought of eating a piece of fruit seemed like hard work.

'Where have you been?'

The room was dark but I recognised her groggy voice.

'Working, I got a job.'

'Where?' she enquired, her bed creaking as she sat up.

'The Gazebo.' There was a pause in the conversation. 'You sorted things out with him?' I asked, just for something to say.

'Oh Rick, yes that was nothing. We've forgotten about it already.'

I don't know who fell asleep first but I awoke still wearing my work clothes.

My second day at The Gazebo and Ron, short for Veronica, the maître d', had called in ill. She was still away on Thursday when a new waitress named Jane started. As Jane had a great deal of experience in the hospitality industry, there was no need to explain anything. Already I could see her efficient manner was going to make my life easier.

‘So, what time do we have our meal break?’ Jane asked Gino, the manager. Astounded by the question, he shrugged his shoulders. ‘Then I’ll take mine at two and Elizabeth can have hers at three. Tomorrow, we’ll swap over.’

After the lunch crowd had dispersed, Jane asked Chef to prepare her a sandwich. When he started protesting, she offered to make it herself.

‘No, I will not have people messing about in my kitchen,’ he snapped, and began to fill her order.

‘If you want something from the menu,’ she told me, ‘make sure Chef knows before he switches off the equipment.’ I explained that I couldn’t possibly afford lunch, not at those prices. ‘But you don’t pay for it,’ she laughed. ‘A meal provided by the establishment is a condition of employment.’

After a long but enjoyable day’s work, I walked into another row between the couple ones. I could hear their raised voices from behind the closed bathroom door.

Amidst this uproar, the big girl was filing her nails and the student, writing in her diary.

‘I’m desperate to go,’ I told them, wondering if I should just knock.

‘Angie,’ the big girl’s voice boomed, ‘Elizabeth needs to use the loo.’

But it wasn’t necessary, for just as she spoke, Rick emerged from the bathroom, pushing past me and out the door.

Switching off the light, I joined them in the room. The big girl broke the strained silence.

‘Well, if you want my opinion, I reckon you’re better off without him.’

‘Oh, he’s not that bad Fiona. It’s her, she’s always there.’

‘His missus?’

They’re divorced but Kate’s been calling. He’s going to see her tomorrow. That’s why he breaks it off with me. He does it every time he visits.’

First thing Saturday morning, I took a bag of washing to the laundromat and called Michael from the payphone. He invited me around. I had met Michael at the newsagents on my first day here. He had pointed out the papers with the best job listings and we had swapped phone numbers.

‘Have you had breakfast?’ he asked, looking at his watch before leading the way to the kitchen. As he rummaged through the pantry, crammed full with ingredients, I guessed that Michael liked to cook. ‘So, how’s the job hunting going?’ he enquired, once the eggs were on the stove. While Michael turned his attention to the fridge, in search of the juice, I quickly told him about The

Gazebo. 'That's great,' he agreed, taking out two plates and placing them on the benchtop. 'Can you grab that toast? I'm thinking we'll eat outside.'

One hour became two, and eventually I left his place around midday, stopping to pick up my laundry before returning to the room.

Opening the door, a wall thick with nicotine greeted me. This was usually a sure sign that Angie was awake. While I folded clothes, she raided her diminishing stash of hash and rolled herself a reefer. In between stretches of silence, I learnt that she never knew her father, and her mother was doing time. I didn't ask why and she didn't elaborate. In the midst of our conversation, the hairy one appeared, sniffed the air, then frowning, locked herself in the bathroom.

When Fiona returned, she too took a short puff and then a longer one. Drawing back on what was now little more than a butt, she accidentally dropped it on the duvet. However, a few quick hits with her palm extinguished the smouldering cotton. By now Fiona had become quite animated, mimicking the old boys at the club where she worked as a barmaid. Midway through an anecdote the hairy one interrupted, made some comment about privacy, then abruptly left.

'What does Brigit do in that bathroom?' Fiona asked. 'You can never hear water running or the toilet flushing. I didn't even know she was there.'

From the moment I first arrived, I'd taken to regularly checking the time, and it was the same today, over and over again. The daylight hours dragged but the nights passed by in a flicker, and it seemed that my head had barely touched the pillow when the sun began streaming in.

This morning, after showering and dressing, I joined the long queue, patiently waiting, before helping myself to tea and toast. I was slowly becoming more comfortable with sharing my personal space. While the bedroom could be locked and I had my own key, it was still communal, along with the dining room, lounge and corridors in between.

Today, after eating breakfast, I found myself a seat, facing the window, just for a change of view. In the background the television was blaring and reporting the news headlines. Despite high unemployment, the civil service was being reduced. Suddenly the snappy man from the other day jumped to his feet and started screaming, the only distraction from the tedium now drowned out by his ranting and raving.

Back in the room, Fiona was filing her nails, the student was writing in her diary, Angie was popping pills so, with nothing else to do, I kicked off my shoes and, slipping under the covers, went back to sleep.

10 June 1984

The females seem to be coexisting quite well. The subjects are rattus norvegicus domestica. These rats tend to be used in laboratories because they are even-tempered.

I have named the newcomer "Australia" because she was the last one to be discovered and included in the experiment's first phase. Already she appears to be forming a bond with a doe that spends much of her time sleeping or grooming.

By and large, the bucks have also been accepting of their surrounds. The only exceptions are the two oldest males. One is becoming quite agitated for no apparent reason, while the other is pacing. These two appear to be spending most of their time in the connecting tunnels, or group feeding areas, so perhaps they are becoming confused or even feel threatened by the scent of the others.

The younger males that were desexed and fitted with testicular implants are still displaying masculine behaviour—not in terms of fighting or biting but through their interest in the females.

For the second phase of the study, I have started increasing the number of subjects. New tunnels now lead to some additional cages, all with occupants. Already the recently introduced subject I've named "Australia" has started visiting these newer parts of the colony.

One of the does, however, is still spending much of her time by the water container. She is not drinking more than the others but appears to need the security of knowing that water is readily accessible. As she was the runt of her litter, it is reasonable to assume that getting food and drink may have been difficult for her in the past, hence her almost territorial approach to the water source in her cage.

Chapter 2

As I arrived at The Gazebo this morning, Ron was back. She and Jane had been introduced and were already at each other. Standing side by side they looked surprisingly similar. If Jane had straight hair, they'd practically pass for twins.

'I don't want the shelves stocked like this,' Ron snapped.

'It doesn't matter what you want,' Jane explained. 'It's Chef who has to work in this kitchen and he prefers it this way.'

Ron turned to Chef for support but instead he shrugged.

For the rest of the morning, they managed to stay away from each other until it came time for me to have my meal break. I asked Chef for a salad and he nodded, bringing it to the table at the back of the room.

'What do you think you're doing?' Ron demanded, rushing up to where I was sitting.

'It's my meal break,' I answered, and proceeded to eat.

'No, it's not,' Ron snapped. 'Since when do you have a meal break?'

'It's part of the conditions,' Jane interrupted, 'a break and a meal provided by the establishment. I'm surprised you didn't know that.'

When it came time for Jane to have her meal, Chef joined her. From their chatting and occasional laughter, it was obvious they'd become friendly. Their camaraderie only served to infuriate Ron all the more.

Next morning, Tom stopped me as I was walking out the door.

'Have you got a minute?' he asked. I was already a little late but let him follow me out to the street. 'Look I don't know if you've heard but they're increasing the numbers here. We're each getting an extra roommate.'

'How can they do that? Where will they sleep?'

'Do you have any single beds in your room?' I nodded, thinking of Brigit's. 'Well, they plan to swap that for a bunk. It's another 35 pounds a week per room, which equates to 1,000s more in profit.'

'What time do you call this?' Ron asked, as I arrived for work. 'Your pay will be docked one hour. Now hurry up!' she ordered.

'I'm not an hour late. You can only dock me 15 minutes.'

'You're paid by the hour and not a minute less.'

Jane was in the kitchen chatting to Chef when I entered. They looked up and smiled.

'She's cutting my pay because I'm a little late,' I explained.

'It's just a threat,' Chef remarked. 'She has no say over salaries. It's Gino who decides how much you're paid. Anyway, if she went to him and made a complaint, he'd probably show her the door. I think he's had enough of her outbursts.'

Friday, Ron and Jane were having words when I walked into The Gazebo. Putting my things away, Chef handed me a cup of freshly brewed coffee and I thanked him. Over the past week, Chef had become quite amiable, even chatty, and I suspected that Jane was the reason.

Leaving The Gazebo that night, Queensway was a fusion of fast-food aromas and middle eastern spices, with local patrons and tourists spilling onto the pavement. In between the mumble of people gathering to relax at the end of the working week, chants of "Support the miners" could be heard from the tube station. There, a few collectors were trying to score small change from the throng of commuters who, with hands in pockets and heads turned down, quickened their pace as they passed. Kensington Gardens was also attracting bigger numbers than usual with couples cuddling on park benches, or laying on the grass.

Everyone seemed to be in pairs this evening except me, of course, and Fiona. She was sitting in the room alone, smoking a cigarette as I threw my bag onto the bed.

'She's gone,' she said, pointing to Angie's made bunk.

Hearing the sound of a key in the door, we turned. But rather than Angie, it was only Brigit, her face twisted into a scowl.

'Do you two ever go out?' she snapped.

'I've just got back,' I replied, but she was already in the bathroom and closing the door.

When Brigit reappeared, she switched off the light. I hadn't even eaten. However, not wanting an argument, I undressed and hopped into bed.

Monday morning, I made my way down to the dining room for toast and tea. I realised that I'd been here too long, when I went back for seconds. Tom said hello and asked me about my job. He seemed pleased for me and I wished that he too would find something to fill his days.

'Six minutes, 38 seconds late,' Tom's friend informed me, as he pointed towards the red double decker bus that had pulled into the kerb.

That evening, everyone was in bed and the lights were out when I opened the door to the room. Stumbling in the dark, I managed to make my way to the bunk.

'Hi,' Fiona whispered, rolling over to face me.

'You're not asleep?'

'Are you kidding? Brigit drew the drapes and turned out the lights at eight. If Angie were here, she wouldn't dream of doing it.'

After so many early nights in a row, I was ready for work before dawn and down in the dining room. Tom was the first to arrive, his skin glowing from a good scrub. Tom never had a hair out of place, always short back and sides. The Busman followed closely behind. He too was clean and tidy in his blue woollen jumper he wore regardless of the weather. Next arrived a man I'd often seen sitting in the corridor. He was 20-something with blonde hair, clean-shaven face, small delicate features and always the same scarf, seemingly flung but really painstakingly placed. The snappy man turned up as well. He was much older than the others, possibly in his mid-50s. He too, was neatly dressed in conservative attire. Whether it was Angie applying her make-up or Fiona filing her nails, it seemed that everyone took care of their appearance. All, of course, except Rick. There he stood with t-shirt hanging out of his crumpled jeans, odd socks and worn running shoes. His eyes were red with dark circles, his hair was in need of a good brush and, by the stubble on his face, it was obvious he hadn't used a razor for days.

'Hi,' he muttered, taking a seat beside me.

'Aren't you going to have some toast?' I asked. 'You'll waste away to nothing.'

'No, tea's fine,' he answered, stirring in three sugars, before adding three more.

Emerging on the opposite side of Kensington Gardens, I was surprised to hear a car horn tooting. It was Jane and Chef. By the look of things, Chef must have gone over to Jane's place after work.

'Hop in,' Jane called, reaching over to unlock the back door.

‘We’re all going to be late this morning,’ Chef noted, now trying to turn against the traffic. ‘Ron will have to threaten the three of us with pay cuts and I’d like to see her do that.’

At The Gazebo we quickly set off in different directions, figuring it would be more difficult for Ron to yell at us if we weren’t all together. As it turned out, we needn’t have bothered.

Soon afterwards, Gino entered the kitchen. He told us that Ron’s father had passed away and she’d gone home to be with her family.

The rest of the day went without a hitch. Jane, Chef and I handled the large crowd of diners easily. We even had time to sit down together for our meal break, after the lunch customers had left.

By evening, the restaurant was almost filled to capacity. We were kept on our toes rushing back and forth to the kitchen with orders and dishes.

As I left that night, Michael was waiting in his car. He had been in Portugal on a photographic shoot. We had some Irish Coffees at his place before he dropped me off with a date for Saturday night.

Brigit’s lights-out curfew continued for the rest of the week. Fiona was now helping herself to Angie’s sleeping pills and I had given up trying to eat in the dark.

Friday, I awoke with a headache. Tom was busy reading the instructions for the model I’d given him under the guise that I needed his help in putting it together. He bombarded me with questions but I explained that I had to get to work.

The last day of the week was generally busy and today was no exception. The bustling crowd of office workers started arriving at midday and stayed until late afternoon. As Jane and I cleared away the tables, I couldn’t help noticing how cheery she was.

Returning to the kitchen to stack the dishwasher, I looked at Chef, or Albert, as Jane was now calling him. He was a little plump with thinning hair and an open, pleasant face. Jane playfully pinched him on the bottom as she moved past, to which he fondly grabbed her hand and gave it a squeeze.

Come closing, Gino announced that Ron would be staying with her Mum for a while.

‘I told her to take her time,’ he continued. ‘I’m assuming that’s okay with you.’

'Well, if you want us to handle the extra work, you'll need to hire a cleaner,' Jane said, pointing to the restrooms.

Gino nodded.

Arriving back and opening the door to the room, I was relieved to see the light on. Brigit was in bed facing the wall, Fiona was filing her nails, Judith was writing in her diary and Angie was holding court. I tossed my bag onto the bunk, kicked off my shoes then, grabbing a piece of fruit, settled in to listen.

17 June 1984

While I have grouped rats in same sex cages, one of the bucks appears to have developed a bond with the docile female. Most nights they can be found huddled together.

Unlike all the other bucks that were neutered when young, this male has not had his testes removed. He was chosen for the experiment because of his curiosity during the selection process. However, due to his age (he has already sired a litter), I decided against desexing and instead opted for chemical castration.

As clinical tests have shown, the chemical microsphere, I chose, suppresses testosterone and, in doing so, eliminates aggression sometimes evident in fertile males.

This chemical injection was delivered subcutaneously to inactivate the testes. Its effects are temporary and it will not prevent this buck from impregnating a female again in the future.

Since the injection, however, the buck could be described as submissive. The docile female even appears to be dominating him at times. The other day, the chemically castrated male was found in another cage at the very far end of the colony. I took the opportunity to extract bloods to ascertain the level of testosterone. The results received today were negative, indicating that his testes have remained inactive and there is still no risk of him impregnating any of the does.

While this buck was being tested, I also removed the docile female from her cage. She has been sleeping for excessively long periods so a health check was warranted. A blood test showed chemicals typically associated with ink. This implies that she may be eating the newspaper used for bedding and this could be the reason for her drowsiness.

When she was being handled, she bit my finger to break free and then ran behind the cabinet. I did not attempt to move the furniture for fear of hurting her.

The docile doe has since somehow returned to the colony. It's a disturbing development, indicating that one of the cages or interconnecting tunnels is not secure.

Chapter 3

I awoke to the sounds of Rick and Angie talking, giggling and then talking again. As I stretched my arms and yawned, it seemed like everything was back to normal. I glanced at Fiona's bed, it was empty and it didn't look as though Judith was in the top bunk. I checked the time; it was already after 11. Kicking off the duvet and slipping my legs out, I sat up and stretched again.

'Good morning,' I heard Rick say and next his head appeared upside down, hanging from the top bunk.

'Hi,' I said, yawning again.

'We didn't wake you?' Angie asked.

'No, I had to get up anyway,' I answered, finally standing.

I wandered off to the bathroom, pleased to see that Brigit wasn't around. As I neared the door, I saw a note on the floor: *Elizabeth, Michael called. He'll pick you up at seven.*

Having showered and dried my hair, I quickly dressed. Rick and Angie were still in bed, totally engrossed in each other. It was good to see them both happy. My bed clothes needed changing, so I carried the pile of crumpled linen downstairs to dump into the laundry bag.

'There you are Elizabeth.' I turned to see Tom and smiled. 'That model's coming along. It's going to be a real beauty. Do you want to see it?' he asked.

Grabbing some fresh linen, I walked into the lounge where Tom, Busman and the snappy man were now gathered around the replica galleon.

In the lounge I could see the regulars, some chatting, others reading but most staring at the screen, as a panel of political analysts pondered the cost of the economic summit.

'What about your timetable?' I asked Busman, surprised to see him away from his post.

‘The next one’s not due for 12 minutes,’ Busman answered, looking at his watch. ‘I’m just helping Tom.’

‘I didn’t ask for your help,’ Tom exclaimed.

‘Well, you didn’t know how to glue the mast,’ Busman continued.

‘I glued the mast, not you,’ the snappy man said.

My mouth dropped open. Up until now I had only been privy to his manic outbursts. Yet here he was making perfect sense.

‘Yes, that’s right Larry. You glued the mast,’ Tom said. ‘Anyway Elizabeth, what do you think so far?’

‘Wonderful,’ I replied. ‘It looks terrific.’ The three of them smiled proudly.

‘Well, we must get on with it, still a lot to be done,’ Busman added.

Walking past the payphone, I reached into my pocket and pulled out some change. I tried Michael’s number, but there was no reply.

Hanging up I tried again, thinking I might have dialled a wrong digit. Again, there was no answer. I made the decision to leave early and walk to Michael’s. That way, he won’t have to come here.

For the next hour or so, I busied myself with domestic duties, making my bed, going to the supermarket and laundromat. I treated myself to a bite of lunch while my washing was being done.

Returning back to the room, I dumped the heavy load of clean laundry on my bed, along with a small bag of groceries, then sat down to catch my breath.

‘What time is it?’ Angie asked, sitting on the top bunk, enjoying a joint with Rick.

‘Just after five,’ I answered. ‘Fiona isn’t back?’

‘Oh, she came in about 20 minutes ago, got changed and rushed out. I think she’s seeing someone,’ Angie said, with a drug-induced slur in her voice.

As Angie and Rick slowly became more stoned, I put away my washing and chose something to wear for my night out with Michael. I was about to slip into my dress, when suddenly the door burst open.

Brigit glared at me fleetingly before rushing to the bathroom in yet another one of her rages. She had left the door to the room ajar, giving anyone who happened to walk by a full view of my semi-naked body. I took a deep breath to repress my annoyance then, dressed only in a black bra and panties, walked over to shut the door. Just as I placed my hand on the door knob, Michael appeared out of nowhere. By the startled look on his face, I had taken him by surprise.

'Come in,' I said, grabbing his arm before closing the door behind him. 'Brigit left the door wide open,' I explained. 'Why are you here so early?'

'Early? I said six and it's six,' he answered, perusing the room, his eyes stopping on Rick and Angie in the top bunk.

I looked to see what had distracted him. The bedding had become dishevelled to reveal Angie's and Rick's naked bodies entwined in a jumble of limbs, the persistent creaking of the springs accompanied by whispered groans.

'That's Angie my roommate and her boyfriend Rick,' I said, feeling it only right I introduce them.

At the mention of their names, Angie and Rick turned their heads and smiled.

'Hi,' they said in unison, the creaking of the springs momentarily stopping.

Michael nodded.

'Brigit's in the bathroom,' I continued. 'She's a bit strange so I won't introduce you. Fiona sleeps in this bed and Judith's in that one.'

Michael's eyes scanned the room and then returned to Rick and Angie. He seemed mesmerised by the action in the top bunk, so I took this opportunity to pop on my dress and slip on my shoes.

'I'm ready,' I announced, making my way to the door.

On seeing me leaving, Michael hurried along. As we walked the length of the corridor, Michael seemed to be deep in thought. 'The message said seven, that's why I thought you were early,' I explained.

'I don't believe it,' he answered.

'Well, it's easy enough done, especially with the number of phone messages they get here.'

'No, not that,' he said, 'them back there, Angie and Rick.'

'Oh,' I replied, hoping he'd leave it at that.

Nothing more was said until we were driving. 'Where are we going?' I asked, not recognising any of the streets.

'West Hampstead. We're having dinner at David's place. He's an Art Director I work with from time to time. I think you'll like him.'

Finally, the car turned into a winding street lined with identical, terraced houses. David's place was in the midst of renovation but charming all the same. Michael knocked on the front door, as I wiped the soles of my shoes.

'Don't worry about wiping your feet,' David said, on opening the door. 'We're in a bit of a mess, there's plaster dust everywhere.'

'David this is Elizabeth,' Michael announced.

David smiled.

'Come in and meet the others,' he said.

Walking up the hallway, I could hear voices at the back of the house. From where I stood it sounded like a party rather than a quiet dinner.

Eventually we were shown into a large room overlooking a small garden. Faces turned as we entered and a large, friendly mutt bounded towards me. Stroking the dog's fur, I was introduced to seven other people. Their names forgotten the moment they were said. Michael obviously knew everyone in the room and immediately felt at ease in their company. David handed me a glass of wine and passed Michael a beer, as we took our seats on the sofa beside a pile of cardboard boxes.

Initially the conversation revolved around business. Everyone in this room was either employed by an advertising agency, or worked as a supplier to the industry. Eventually the conversation turned to David's renovations, then to Michael's Portugal trip, onto someone else's Hawaiian holiday, before finally returning to the business of advertising.

By the time we sat down to dinner, two hours had passed and I was counting the minutes until we could leave. Between the starter and the main course, Michael finished his fifth beer and refilled the glass. Surprisingly he didn't seem to be any worse the wear for the amount of alcohol he'd consumed. By this stage the conversation had turned to some woman who'd been arrested at Piccadilly Circus for streaking past the constabulary. The dinner guests laughed as David told his account of the story, while mimicking the reactions of the passers-by.

'That's nothing,' Michael interrupted. 'Tell them about Angie and Rick,' he suggested, nudging me in the arm. Everyone focused their eyes on me expecting an hilarious anecdote, but instead I didn't respond. 'I'll tell them,' Michael decided, ignoring my hand suddenly squeezing his arm. 'Elizabeth lives in this amazing place. This old, tumble-down hotel. I went to pick her up tonight and there in her room this couple was doing it, shagging right in front of us.' I squeezed Michael's arm again, desperately hoping he'd stop. But they wanted to know more. 'This Angie is sprawled there stark naked, really tarty looking with all this eye make-up,' he continued. 'On top of her is this guy, stoned out of his brain. But get this, in the middle of it all, Elizabeth's roaming around in her undies acting as if this is nothing out of the ordinary.'

'Why were they in your room?' someone asked.

'No, it's this Angie's room too,' answered Michael. 'There are five of them in this tiny room.'

'Five of you, how can you bear it?' another one enquired.

'But there's more,' Michael added. 'When I arrived, Elizabeth wouldn't introduce me to someone in the bathroom because she's a bit strange. The one in the bathroom's a bit strange. Yet here we are staring at this couple, bonking, and Elizabeth introduces me to them.'

Everyone laughed as Michael took another sip from his beer. I used this brief pause to excuse myself and seek out the bathroom.

As I went from door to door, I could hear bursts of laughter coming from the dining room. Michael was still amusing them with his entertaining recount. Eventually I located the bathroom upstairs. After locking myself in the room, an overwhelming wave of nausea spread through my body. Obviously, nerves. For a second, I thought I would vomit. But it was a false alarm. Lowering the toilet seat, I sat down to steady my legs. I must have stayed in there for more than 10 minutes, checking myself in the bathroom mirror before I returned downstairs. Unfortunately, the conversation was still focused on my living conditions. But the giggles subsided as I took my seat at the table.

'Elizabeth do me a favour?' the man sitting opposite asked. 'Take my Polaroid and get some snaps.'

Again, everyone laughed.

As sweets arrived on the table, the conversation turned to someone called Tanya.

'How is Tanya? I hear she's been offered the Laura Ashley contract,' one of the women remarked.

'Well, her agent is in talks,' Michael answered.

'How's it going with the new man?' the fellow opposite enquired.

'Alastair? Oh, not too well. A few problems,' Michael shrugged, butting out his cigarette and sculling the rest of his glass.

By midnight, we said our good-byes. Michael stumbled a few times on the way to the car so I offered to drive.

'No, I'm fine,' he stated, annoyed that I should suggest otherwise. The trip back was uncomfortably quiet. Not that I wanted to break the silence, I didn't. I had nothing to say to Michael, nothing at all. 'What's the matter?' Michael asked, as we approached Kensington. 'You put out about something?' I stared at him searching for the words. There were none. 'Well? What?' Michael asked, his cocky manner grating on my nerves.

'What do you think, Michael?' I replied, trying to suppress my anger.

'What? The Angie and Rick story? It's a laugh. So what?'

'You run down my friends, you make fun of me and I shouldn't be put out. Who in the hell do you think you are?'

'Listen don't you take that high and mighty tone with me,' he snapped. 'I'm not the freak here. How can you exist like that? You must be sick or something.'

Suddenly Michael slammed his foot on the brake, narrowly avoiding the car in front which had abruptly stopped. I didn't waste any time. Opening the door, I jumped out of the car and sped off down the road. Luckily, I was only five minutes or so from home. I ran through the streets without stopping, until I arrived breathless at The Elms.

Stumbling inside, I sat down, a fit of coughing prompted by this burst of physical exertion.

'Do you often go jogging dressed like that?'

Turning I saw the smug 20-something with the trademark scarf sitting in the armchair, the glowing tip of his cigarette the only light apart from the exit sign that shone above the doorway.

'What?'

'Well, you're either jogging or being chased. Which one is it?' he asked, with an unappealing assuredness.

'Neither,' I said, as I walked towards the stairs.

Unlocking the door to my room, I was relieved to see that Brigit had gone out. I wasn't in the mood for any of her curt remarks. Instead, Angie and Rick smiled at me, as they sat on the top bunk chatting to Fiona.

'Did you have a good night?' Angie asked, as I dropped my bag on the bed.

I nodded.

'He seemed nice,' Rick remarked.

'Where'd you go?' Fiona enquired. 'You look pretty, new dress?'

'Another time,' I said. 'I'm feeling a bit nauseous. Had a little too much to drink.'

It was well after midday when I awoke. Thankfully only Fiona was in the room, sitting on her bed, staring.

'Good afternoon,' she said, still gazing, her spectacled eyes unblinking.

'Hi,' I answered, rubbing my brow and squinting to block out the sunlight.

'Heavy night, eh? Want to tell me about it?' I shook my head. 'Well, if it's any consolation Michael's very sorry.' I looked at her not really understanding. 'He's very sorry,' she repeated. 'It says so on the flowers,' she added, pointing across to the chest of drawers. There standing amongst the pile of groceries was a bunch of roses. I sat up to see more clearly, my vision not having fully adjusted to the light pouring into the room. 'The note wasn't in an envelope, so I read it. Hope you don't mind?'

'No, that's okay,' I answered, letting my head fall back onto the pillow. 'What does it say?'

'It says: "Elizabeth, I acted like a prize cock. I could blame the alcohol but I've been drunk before and never behaved that badly. I can't tell you how sorry I am. Please forgive me, Michael." And then there's a big X. So, what happened?'

'Oh, we had a fight. He said that I was living like a stray. I was weird or something.'

'If he thinks you're weird, wait until he meets Brigit or that fascist downstairs.'

'What fascist?' I asked.

'Oh, you know him, he's always hanging around, fair hair, wears a scarf. Are you going to forgive Michael?'

'No, don't think I could. He's not for me.' Then after a pause: 'So, what about you, seeing anyone?' My question caught Fiona off guard.

'Yes, well sort of, Julian, but no future there either. He's 50 and married. You should put those roses in water. There's an old jar over there.'

24 June 1984

The doe I named "Australia" has been seen with a wild rattus rattus. The buck was even observed in the doe's cage. There have been instances when colonies of rats have welcomed outsiders with few issues, apart from the odd territorial spat usually to determine the alpha male. That said, of course, this situation is less than ideal.

Having street rats mixing with the test subjects raises concerns with regard to the spread of contaminants, such as flees, and the risk of disease. Both of which could impact the behaviour of the colony inhabitants, in terms of submission, aggression or general wellbeing.

This wild rattus rattus also appears to be attracting other wild rats. In one of the disused cages, that was undergoing repairs, I have noticed rat droppings. I will include this development as a trial protocol amendment, until such time as I can identify how rats are entering and escaping the colony.

To this end, population growth will now not only be confined to chosen subjects but may include intrusive participants. While this is not a model situation, it is seen to be a more suitable solution than abandoning the experiment altogether, or deferring it until all cages can be emptied and fully inspected.

Another development is that some of the bucks appear to be hoarding. While it is common for rats to hoard food, these bucks appear to be busying themselves with a stash of small objects made from wood, plastic and other non-edible materials. As it is still summer, it is unlikely these rats are feeling the cold and are creating extra bedding. Instead collecting objects could be a sign of anxiety, in much the same way that humans sometimes start hoarding as a result of trauma, stress or depression.

Chapter 4

Monday, I was awoken by Angie, holding a piece of paper.

'What's that?' I asked.

'It's the name of an art school. They need a life model.'

'Give them a call.'

'Already have. I'm going to see them later today. Do you think you could come with me?' I nodded and she gave my hand a squeeze.

Downstairs, Tom waved and called for me to join him. He was sitting with Busman and another fellow I hadn't seen before, though there were so many new faces around The Elms these days.

'Model's coming along nicely,' Tom told me, as soon as I was within ear shot.

'It's cumbersome to carry around now,' Busman added. 'So, it's been set up in Tom's room on a piece of hardboard.'

I smiled and then turned to their companion.

'Elizabeth, do you know Jasper?' Tom asked.

'Hello,' I said. 'I haven't seen you before.'

'No, just moved in,' he answered.

I looked at Jasper. His smooth complexion with the odd trace of black, fluffy, hair growth made him appear pubescent. In reality, he was probably in his mid-20s. Tom seemed positively taken by him and he, in turn, was relishing the attention. Despite having just met, it was obvious they liked each other.

'Jasper's here because of the miner's strike. Trying to raise some money for bail,' Tom explained, almost yelling with exuberance. He noticed me staring and blushed.

'You know after what's just happened at Orgreave,' Jasper continued. 'You must have seen it on the news. Crowds of pickets have been arrested and some of these charges can get life but they're not criminals, just working, family men trying to put food on the table.'

'Should look at collecting at Kensington South tube station, maybe Gloucester Road also,' Busman added. 'Though a lot of people are doing it tough. So, you might not even cover your rent, let alone raise enough to help those back home.'

'Did you work for London Transport?' I asked Busman, taking him by surprise. By the way Tom dropped his head, and proceeded to scratch his scalp, I knew I shouldn't have pried.

'You weren't to know Elizabeth,' Tom said, after Busman and Jasper had excused themselves. 'Bob was a factory foreman and a fella was killed on his shift. Apparently, Bob had been complaining that equipment needed replacing, but the bosses wouldn't listen. At first, he hit the bottle. He's over that now. But his confidence has taken a battering. That's the trouble with the people here, we've all lost our spirit. After a while, you're too scared to leave. You've lost touch with the outside world, the little things like gardening, cooking, keeping a house clean. It's daft but that's what happens. Now don't you go getting like that. You get out of here as soon as you can and travel like you planned.'

The art school was in Kilburn. For the first leg, Angie scored a seat on the tube and proceeded to reapply her make-up. I stood by the door. The second leg was a crowded bus. We temporarily lost each other but once we hit Shoot Up Hill, the bus had almost emptied so we could sit side by side. At this point I noticed what Angie was wearing. She had on a short, skin tight, red dress with black stockings and stilettos. Snake-like bangles curled their way up both arms. She wore more make-up than usual. Or perhaps it was just the flash of red lipstick, a shade I'd not seen her wear before.

'It's just up this street,' Angie pointed, and we prepared to disembark.

The art school had been a church in a former life. Inside we were greeted by the smell of fresh paint, obviously coming from the whiter than white walls. The floor was sanded. There were easels and a few chairs haphazardly stacked in the centre of the room. Seeing no one around, we ventured further inside, Angie's heels thundering on the bare boards.

'Can I help you?' Our heads turned to see a stocky man with a greying beard and unruly white hair. Dressed casually in a denim shirt and jeans he entered the room, careful not to trip on the white sheets he was carrying. After casually dumping his load on one of the seats, he repeated his question. 'Can I help you?'

'I rang before. Did I speak to you?' Angie asked. He looked at her blankly. 'About the job. Life model?' she continued.

'Oh yes, you did speak to me. Karen, wasn't it?'

'Angie,' she corrected.

'Well, take a seat, I'll be with you in a minute,' he gestured, gathering the sheets and roughly folding them, before storing them in a cupboard at the far end of the room. 'We're still in a bit of a mess,' he explained, walking back to where we were seated. 'Classes don't start until later this week.'

'Oh,' Angie said, crossing her legs and sitting upright before taking a moment to joosh up her hair.

'Now have you done modelling before?' he asked, plonking his body down and pulling a notebook from his back pocket.

'I did a clothes store catalogue when I was a child. I was about nine,' Angie recalled.

'No, life modelling,' he explained, now leaning sideways to balance his notebook on the armrest.

'Oh,' Angie laughed. 'No, I've never done life modelling. I've been an exotic dancer though, at Wickham's Bar in Soho. You know it?'

He shook his head.

'Well life modelling is a little different because you're not moving around, you need to stand still. We usually have a short break every quarter of an hour so you can stretch your legs, have a coffee, that sort of thing, and then we resume. Classes last approximately two hours. At the moment it's quite warm in here, but there'll be a small heater in case it turns chilly. These places can be draughty. Well, that's about it. Any questions?' he enquired.

'How much does it pay?' Angie asked.

'Twenty pounds a class and you'll be required for two to four classes a week. We use other models as well so some weeks you may have four sessions, other weeks you might only be needed for two. You get paid after each class and the tutor will have the money.'

'Sounds good,' Angie replied, turning to me and nodding.

'Then I'll get your details,' he stated. 'Just write down your name, address and phone number and we'll contact you about your session times.' Angie scribbled down the information and passed the notebook back. 'Well, that's that,' he said, standing. 'Oh, by the way, my name's Lewis, I'm one of the tutors. I'll see you in class.'

'He seemed friendly enough,' Angie commented, once we were outside. 'A professor I'm guessing. Can't wait to tell Rick, he will be so chuffed for me.'

Arriving back at The Elms, Angie ventured off to find Rick and give him the good news.

I took my time walking to the room, thinking that maybe I would take a nap. No sooner had I opened the door than my attention turned to the roses that were scattered over the floor. Assuming the jar had been blown off the window sill, I walked over to pick them up. As I approached the bed, my eyes darted to a piece of white paper lying on top of the quilt: *Get your own jar. Brigit.*

I was sitting on my bunk bed with message in hand when Angie and Rick returned to the room

'Great news isn't it, Elizabeth?' Rick remarked. 'We should celebrate.'

'What's that?' Angie said, craning her neck to read Brigit's handwriting. 'God she's a bitch,' she commented, passing the note to Rick.

'Listen I've got a jar in my room; I'll go and get it.'

For the remainder of the day I slept, dozing off for an hour or so, eating a little and then dozing off again. Angie and Rick chatted on the top bunk, drinking some beer they'd bought to toast the new job.

That night, I tossed and turned, waking then drifting off again every hour or so. I was up, showered and dressed well before the others yet, despite my energetic start, exhausted none the less.

Venturing downstairs for breakfast, I found myself in the company of Busman. He was more cheerful than yesterday morning and seemed genuinely pleased to see me.

'Good morning, Elizabeth. You're up bright and early. Don't often see you down here at this time.'

'No, didn't sleep well,' I answered, grabbing four pieces of toast.

'I know the feeling,' he replied, pouring tea into my mug and then into his.

'You've had trouble sleeping too? Maybe it's the weather.'

'No, I've never slept well, Insomnia. I've just learnt to live with it.'

After seating ourselves at a table, we resumed our conversation.

'Haven't seen Larry around. Has he left?' I enquired, taking a bite of my toast.

'No, he's up in his room.'

'Is he ill?' I asked.

'No, he's having one of his moods. Once you've lived with Larry for a while, you come to accept that he has these moods. He can get a bit nasty. But most of the time he's withdrawn and timid, frightened of anything and everyone.'

Busman stopped to take a sip and I waited for him to continue. ‘When he’s like this he stays in his room. He’s been known to spend a week up there, hiding under his bed.’

‘Do you think he’ll be okay? Shouldn’t we check that he’s all right?’

‘No, he’ll be fine. He wants to be left alone. When he’s feeling this way, it’s best to give him his space.’

28 June 1984

Having just increased the number of occupants again, I am concerned to see what appears to be the start of a nest in one of the doe cages. Flowers and twigs are on the floor.

Care has been taken to prevent impregnation for two reasons: Firstly; a litter could produce up to 14 new subjects, significantly boosting a cage's population prematurely. Even though we are increasing the number of participants, it is important that we maintain control over the quantity to more accurately assess any impacts. Secondly; at the observation stage of the study, does were not monitored with pups. So, we would be totally reliant on previous documentation in analysing antenatal and maternal responses.

The cage in question is the one where the doe "Australia" was seen with a rattus rattus from outside the experiment. However, if this is a nest, it would suggest that gestation is nearing completion and impregnation would have taken place around 21 days ago, well before the two were sighted together.

As a result of this latest development, the does in this cage are being closely monitored for any signs of pregnancy. To date, there have been no obvious weight gains. No increase in appetite. Nor any other physical indications such as a mucous plug in the vagina, swollen abdomen or protruding nipples among these subjects.

So, while it is rare for rats to have phantom pregnancies, it appears that this could be the case here and, as such, this development will be noted as a behavioural change.

Chapter 5

Stepping out of The Elms, I noticed Michael's car parked in the kerb.

'Elizabeth,' he called. I snubbed him. 'I'll give you a lift,' he persevered. I hastened my step. Crossing the road, I became lost in the crowd of commuters that swept me towards the next corner. Waiting at the lights, a car suddenly screeched to a halt. 'Get in,' Michael said, abruptly opening the passenger door. 'Get in,' he repeated more forcibly when I failed to respond. The lights changed and I crossed the road, walking around Michael's car, along with the other pedestrians.

Entering Kensington Gardens I slowed to a more leisurely stroll, confident that he couldn't drive up one of the pathways. The gardens were filled with energetic people; some jogging, others walking their dogs, a small group was doing T'ai Chi and a family was playing with a frisbee. It came my way and I threw it back. Emerging from the gateway on the Bayswater border, I caught sight of Michael's car idling by the roadside.

'Are you going to get in or do I have to follow you all the way to work?' he called, his head poking out of the opened car window. I continued to ignore him, maintaining an easy stride. As I reached Queensway, I could still sense Michael's car crawling along behind me. It was beginning to get on my nerves. 'Elizabeth, come on. Don't be so stubborn,' I heard him call. I stopped and turned around.

'Look Michael, I've got to get to work. Just leave me alone, okay?'

Arriving at The Gazebo, I had no time to worry about Michael.

'Can you help Jane grab the Christmas trees?' Gino called, as I walked into the restaurant.

'Christmas trees?' I asked, thinking I had misheard Gino's instructions.

Apparently, we were catering for a company function, a mid-year Yuletide of all things. I found Jane in the back room up to her waist in boxes.

'Can you believe this?' she asked. 'We have to set up all these fake trees and decorate them, on top of everything else. Albert's freaking out. He's expected to prepare a full Christmas feast with three hours' notice. There isn't even an assistant to help with the preparation. Honestly, if they don't employ a kitchen hand soon, Albert will walk out. I don't know how he's lasted this long.'

'He didn't know about the Christmas party?'

'Not until he arrived an hour ago. It really is unforgivable.'

Lugging the boxed Christmas trees out to the restaurant, Gino ordered that we drop them on the floor, telling us that the company was sending someone to decorate them.

'There are candles in the kitchen. Can you get them Elizabeth? White table cloths in the drawer Jane.'

Separating we hurried in different directions.

'I can't believe that bitch!' Chef fumed, as I walked in and began scouring the shelves before searching through the cupboards.

'Who?' I asked.

'Ron, who else? She's known about this function for weeks, even ordered the supplies. But did she think to tell anyone about it? Write it in the reservations' book? No. If the company hadn't called this morning, we wouldn't have known they were expected today and I would've been wondering why all these turkeys had been delivered. She's a right bitch, that's what she is.'

Already Jane had laid all the cloths, so I busied myself adding two candles to each table.

'Are there going to be place cards?' Jane asked, suddenly realising that we may be required to join some tables together.

'No, I don't think so,' Gino replied, and then, 'oh hell, I don't know.'

'I'll phone them,' Jane suggested. Returning some minutes later, she gave us the bad news. 'There are going to be place cards, they're bringing them.' Gino threw his arms up in the air. 'Don't worry I have the numbers for each table, we can work from that,' Jane stated in her usual organised manner. 'Can you help me move these?'

Gino, Jane and I joined tables to accommodate the number of places that were required in each group. It was heavy work, leaving us thoroughly hot and sweaty. Next condiments and water jugs were placed on each table, along with Christmas napkins and crackers.

'Hello.'

In the midst of our manic preparations, we heard a voice and turning, saw two young women standing at the door.

'Yes?' Gino asked abruptly.

'We've brought the place cards,' one of the girls announced.

'Oh good,' Jane replied. 'I'll leave it to you to put them on the tables. Okay?'

'Well, it'll be easy enough for you to follow,' the girl remarked, keen to pass the task onto someone else.

Jane ignored her suggestion and continued delegating.

'Now while your friend's doing that, you can start on the Christmas trees. Decorations are in that box over there.' The girl looked at her colleague and they grimaced. Jane, ignoring their expressions, disappeared into the kitchen.

'Elizabeth,' I heard Jane calling. I excused myself and joined her. 'Don't let them talk you into decorating those trees,' she remarked, as I appeared. I shook my head.

For the next hour Jane and I assisted Chef in the kitchen. There was so much to do and few hands to help make the load lighter. In the end Gino had his sleeves rolled up, as he joined the production line.

The luncheon guests arrived and proceeded to empty bottle after bottle of wine. By the time the main course had been served, they had consumed double the quantity of alcohol originally requested. The more intoxicated the guests became, the less they cared about the food, with no one noticing that Chef's cooking was slightly under par.

The Christmas party continued well into the night. Not that the guests were expecting dinner, they weren't. Instead, the revellers were content to almost drink our cellar empty. Gino was delighted, alcohol was always more profitable than food. At this rate he would have reached the weekly target in just one day. By 10pm, the last of the guests stumbled into cabs and left us to restore order.

After helping to tidy up, Gino opened a bottle of wine and suggested we all join him for a drink. Laughing and discussing the events of the day, we stayed and drank for hours. It was already well after midnight when Chef and Jane dropped me at the entrance to The Elms.

As soon as I reached my bed, I undressed and collapsed under the covers. The moment my head touched the pillow, I was out cold.

I overslept this morning, not surprising considering the amount of wine I'd had the night before. I wasn't used to drinking that much and my pounding head was assuring me that I'd think twice about it in future. I had missed breakfast but I couldn't have stomached much this morning, not even dry toast and tea.

Arriving at The Gazebo I was pleased to see I wasn't the only one suffering. Everyone was unusually subdued and we went about our business quietly. When Chef dropped a saucepan lid, we all over-reacted. In our fragile conditions, the noise seemed deafening.

Very little was said all day and even less was eaten, each of us passing up our mid-afternoon meal. Come closing we went our separate ways, taking our weary bodies home to bed.

Back in the room Judith and Fiona were making signs for the Gay Pride March.

'Lewis called. Thursday at noon and then again at three,' Angie excitedly told me.

'He called. That's good. When do you start?' I asked, sitting on my bunk to relieve my aching feet.

'I told you, Thursday at noon and then at three,' she responded, as I removed my shoes.

'Two sessions, that's excellent.'

'Yes, 40 pounds. Not bad for half a day's work.' Judith and Fi were now in the bathroom washing the paint from their hands. 'Do you think Fiona's a lesbian?' Angie leant in and whispered in my ear. I shrugged and proceeded to undress. 'I'm only wondering because she hasn't introduced us to that person she's been seeing.' I hung my clothes at the end of the bed. 'I just hope she knows that her girlfriend is welcome here.'

I slid my weary body under the covers and rolled over to face the wall. As Angie continued to talk, I closed my eyes. Her voice seemed to be fading.

Chapter 6

The room was quiet, I guessed that Brigit and Fiona had left for work or were downstairs having breakfast. Judith's bed was also empty. Even though she is a student, I've never seen her study. Apart from writing in her diary, I'm not sure what she does with her days. Of course, I knew that Angie and Rick were still fast asleep in the top bunk. I could tell by the double dip in the mattress.

Being the last in the bathroom, the shower was freezing cold. But thankfully the hair dryer provided some warmth.

I was now running a little late, so I quickly went to grab some clean clothes from the suitcase under my bed. As I bent down on my hands and knees, I noticed a strange odour. I couldn't see anything that would cause the foul smell, but by then it seemed to have dissipated.

'It's probably one of Rick's old socks caught down the side of Angie's bed,' I thought, before sliding the case back in place.

I arrived at The Gazebo on time having sprinted, for the most part, through Kensington Gardens. Gino was in a cheerful mood as I walked in, telling me that the owners were going to refurbish the restaurant. Jane didn't share his positive take on things.

'I can't afford to be without a salary. There's nothing wrong with the place. They're just avoiding tax that's all.'

'Why would you be without money?' I asked.

'Well, they'll close the place while they're renovating and we won't be paid. It's worse than being unemployed because we can't apply for benefits.' Later in the day, as we sat down to our meal, Gino announced that work would start the following week and take 14 days. 'You've already told us that,' Jane interrupted. 'What exactly will they be doing? It looks all right to me.'

'They'll be painting the place right through, new carpets and they're going to replace the tables and chairs.'

'Well, you'd better let Ron know,' I suggested.

'I was going to give her a call anyway. She was expected back last Monday. If she's planning to stay with her mother, for a while longer, at least she could let us know.'

We all nodded.

By dinner time, Jane's mood had improved and she seemed to be looking forward to a break from work. Probably because Chef had suggested they drive to Oxford to stay with some of his friends, then call in to see his family on the way back to London.

Looking at Chef, I couldn't imagine him ever having been a child, let alone someone's baby. I was just about to ask him about his family, when Jane barged into the kitchen.

'That fella's in the restaurant,' she said, placing an order on the spike.

'What fella?' I asked.

'The one you went out with. He drove you home,' she explained, collecting two meals and carefully balancing them on her arms, before picking up the third and fourth.

I rushed to peek through the swing door. 'I can't see him,' I said.

'Well hold the door open for me and have a look as I go out.'

Following Jane's suggestion, I saw Michael sitting in the far corner on one of my allocated tables.

'Why'd you put him on my table?' I asked Jane, as soon as she reappeared.

'I didn't, Gino did,' she replied, picking up two carafes of water before disappearing into the restaurant again.

'Food's ready for table nine,' Chef announced, removing the next orders from the spike and laying them out in front of him. Juggling the dishes laden with hot food, I took a deep breath before entering the restaurant. I tried not to look in Michael's direction as I delivered the food to table nine, served table eight and returned to the kitchen with the orders. I carried out a cheese and fruit platter to table four, took their order for drinks and again escaped to the kitchen. Emerging I carried sweets to table six, wrote down an order for coffees and was about to return to the kitchen, when I heard my name called. Turning I saw Michael sitting with his arms folded, looking decidedly peeved.

'I'll be with you in a moment,' I answered, before taking the last order into Chef and depositing it on the spike. 'Here goes,' I said to myself, walking into the restaurant with notepad in hand and pen poised. 'Now what will it be?' I asked, carefully avoiding Michael's eyes.

'Will you talk to me?' he whispered, so the next table wouldn't hear. 'Just talk to me.'

'Well, you can choose from the menu or from today's specials,' I replied, still looking at my notepad. 'The fish of the day is filleted Sole, stuffed with grapes and baked, lightly basted in a tangy lemon sauce. The soup is pumpkin with…'

'Would you stop it? Just stop it.'

I looked up to see Michael run his fingers through his hair, before sitting back in the chair to stare into my face. His close scrutiny made me uncomfortable and I could feel my skin burning.

'Are you here to eat or not?' I finally asked. 'I don't have all day to stand around.'

'I just want to talk to you for a few minutes,' he explained, his voice so quiet I could hardly hear him. 'After you finish tonight, I just want to talk. That's all. Five minutes.' He paused momentarily, waiting for an answer. 'We can go and get a coffee or…'

'No, I don't want to go anywhere,' I snapped.

'Or, as I was going to say, we could just talk outside.'

'All right. Five minutes,' I answered. 'Now are you going to eat?'

'Yes, the fish will do.'

Michael didn't bother me after that and acted just like any other customer. I served his meal. He ordered a beer. He finished up and asked for the bill. Clearing Michael's table, I noticed he'd left 70 pounds and the rage erupted inside me. Snatching up his plate and glass, I stormed into the kitchen.

'What's up?' Jane asked, sensing my aggravation.

'He left me a 50-pound tip,' I fumed.

I could see by Jane's and Chef's expressions that they didn't understand. If it had been anyone else, I would have been ecstatic but because it was Michael I was seething.

At closing, I farewelled Gino, Jane and Chef then, grabbing my bag, made my way out the door. I saw Michael's car parked outside, but he wasn't seated behind the steering wheel.

'Hi,' I heard behind me and turning saw Michael leaning against the wall. 'What do you want to do, go for a walk, have a coffee or I could drive you home?' he asked, taking a step towards me, his hesitant movements revealing his nervousness.

'Well, you may as well drive me home. I'm tired.'

He nodded and approaching his car proceeded to unlock the door, holding it open as I got in.

Taking his place in the driver's seat he started the engine and then switched it off.

'How about we talk first and then I'll drive you home?'

'Okay, what do you want to say?'

'You got my flowers?' I nodded. 'Well like I said, I'm sorry, really sorry. I've never done that before. I don't know why I did it.' He paused then continued. 'Do you understand what I'm saying?'

'You're sorry,' I repeated, in a matter-of-fact tone.

'Don't you believe me?'

'Yes.'

'So, why are you still angry with me? I don't know what else I can say.'

'There's nothing else to say, you're sorry and I accept your apology. Let's leave it at that.'

'But I don't want to leave it,' he responded, reaching over to touch my hand.

'But I do,' I answered, pulling my hand away.

'Why? Because I stuffed up the once. That's it?'

'You and I are very different. If my friends shock you so much, if my living conditions disgust you, we're obviously not suited. And to be perfectly honest, if you're as worldly as you make out, why would two people shagging be so amazing? I mean it's an everyday act, isn't it?'

'Yes, but you've got to admit, it was a little unusual,' he replied.

'Unusual by whose standards? You have your own bedroom and two others to spare. You think you're the rule, but you're not. In London, you're the exception. Open your eyes. For a photographer, it staggers me that you can't see what's around you. Don't you notice the bag ladies? They're on every second street or do you just assume they go home to their comfy bedsits each night. What about the beggars? Even the miners collecting coins at the tube. Wake up Michael, we're just coming out of a recession, with a housing shortage and high unemployment. The Elms isn't filled with backpackers like me. It's filled with people who live there permanently. That's home, day in day out. There are places like that all over London. So, what if two people are feeling a little horny. Where else are they supposed to go?'

'But it was the afternoon. I mean if you want to do that, you'd wait until night time.'

'Oh, you've never done it in the afternoon, or late morning, or early evening? Anyway, we turn up all hours of the day and night. We all have our own keys. You never have guaranteed privacy. What's the big deal anyway about seeing two people loving each other? I'd much rather see that than someone getting hurt or abused.' Michael looked out the window. 'Oh, by the way, here's your money,' I added, holding out the 50 pounds.

'It was a tip,' he answered, waving his hand in the air.

'So, I served your fish so brilliantly that it deserved a 50-pound tip? I'm not a charity, Michael. What were you going to do, claim it at tax time as a donation to a down and out?'

I placed the 50 pounds on the dashboard and Michael started the engine. During the short drive to The Elms nothing was said, there was no need. When Michael's car pulled into the kerb, I said my good-byes and opened the door to get out.

'Elizabeth, don't stay away. If you want to drop by for coffee, please do. I'm really not as bad as you think.'

Arriving back in the room Angie, Rick and Fiona were awake, chatting to each other from their beds.

'We're trying to work out what this smell is?' Angie commented.

'What smell? I can't smell anything,' I replied, walking towards them. 'Oh hell, now I can. What is it?'

'It smells like a dead animal decomposing,' Fiona remarked, lying back in her bed, filing her nails.

'Rick said something might have died in one of the walls,' Angie added.

'Probably electrocuted,' Rick continued. 'This wall I think,' he stated, tapping the one along the side of my bed.

'Yes, I noticed it this morning,' I remembered. 'I thought it was one of your socks Rick.'

'Oh thanks, they're sometimes a little bit musty, but not that bad.'

Fiona and Angie laughed.

'Hey, you don't think someone's been murdered. Their body cut into small pieces and concealed in the wall?' Fiona piped in, half joking, half serious.

Suddenly there was an ear-piercing scream out in the corridor. Startled, we all jumped then, clutching our chests, listened again. Looking around at each other's stunned faces we laughed out loud. It was a raucous, hearty laughter until our stomach muscles ached from the strain. Even after the laughter had subsided, we continued to giggle intermittently until eventually we went to sleep.

8 July 1984

The wild rattus rattus is moving more freely around the colony. This time the buck was seen in one of the cages that the subjects themselves have turned into a kind of communal eating area.

When we first chose our rat subjects, some came from the same laboratory and therefore had an established relationship of sorts. The others were introduced. Even so, most subjects were accepting of each other. Those who had any issues were removed because, to monitor changes in behaviour, it was vital that all subjects started out being even-tempered.

Usually rats that have been bred together get along very well with few, if any, conflicts. Outsider rats will be accepted but generally this involves a jostling for position, if you like, to establish the social hierarchy. This does not appear to have happened with the intrusive rattus rattus.

Being a wild rat, the buck in question should also be more aggressive and vocal than the test subjects. Again, we have seen no signs of this, quite the opposite.

When observed in the communal eating cage, the wild buck seemed to be quite timid, especially around the doe named "Australia".

Interestingly, none of the buck subjects appear to have noticed the rattus rattus newcomer. Or, if they have, do not feel threatened by his presence. Developments will be monitored.

Of course, there still remains the concern that there is an opening in one of the cages or connecting tunnels that we are yet to find. However, we will remain vigilant.

Chapter 7

This morning in the dining room, I discovered that it had been Larry screaming the night before.

'The manager's right fed up,' Tom announced, over breakfast. 'For three days now, Larry has had the door to his room barricaded and the other fellas he shares with are none too pleased. Sure, they've been given other beds but all their things are back in that room. Apparently, Larry slipped out of the room last night and ran into someone in the hall. So, what did he do? He screamed like a lunatic and then disappeared into his room, been locked in there ever since. If he doesn't behave, they'll call the police. I'm surprised they haven't done that already.'

'What's wrong with him?' I asked.

'It's hard to say Elizabeth, the mind's a strange thing. But there's nothing for you to worry about. I don't think that Larry is a danger to anyone. If anything, he's more of a risk to himself.'

Leaving Tom, I grabbed my bag and made my way out the door. I hadn't seen Angie this morning. I wanted to wish her well. It seemed strange to think of Angie rushing off to work and I was looking forward to hearing all about it later tonight.

My day at The Gazebo was fairly uneventful. An interior decorator was there discussing colour schemes and furnishings with Gino. Being Thursday, it was busy. In fact, the hours sped by. Before I knew it, the last customer had left. Quickly tidying up, we all called it a night as well.

I wasted no time getting to Kensington Gardens. I wanted to see Angie before she went to sleep, hear about her first day at work. The gardens were almost deserted. Instead of walking I sprinted from one side to the other, only stopping briefly to retrieve a hair brush that had fallen from my bag. Arriving at The Elms, I ended up doubled over on the doorstep, gasping.

Still a little breathless, I bypassed the lounge and went directly to my room. I saw my bunk bed had been pulled from the wall. Angie, Rick and Fiona were on their hands and knees, inspecting the plaster.

'What are you guys doing?' I asked.

'We're trying to see if there is any moisture, blood, anything that might hint something is decomposing,' Fiona answered, looking up fleetingly before returning to the task at hand.

'Well, there's definitely something dead in this wall. The smell is putrid,' Rick replied, standing to stretch his legs.

'Well, I can't see anything,' Angie griped, giving up the search and moving away.

'How was your first day?' I asked, walking over to join her on Fiona's bed. 'Phew, it reeks,' I cringed, covering my nose with my hand.

'Yes, you don't notice it when you come in,' Angie remarked. 'But as soon as you walk over here it hits you.'

'That's why it has to be something in this wall,' Rick explained.

'We better complain about it tomorrow, get them to do something,' Fiona suggested, joining Angie and me on the bed.

Rick nodded in agreement and pushing the bunk back, lit himself a cigarette.

'So how was your first day?' I repeated, moving to sit on my own bunk.

'Oh, fine, I think. You sort of don't do much, just stand or sit. They don't really talk to you either. It's like you're not alive.'

'You didn't like it? It sounds great,' I replied, with more enthusiasm than was warranted.

'It's all right. It's a job.'

Sensing that Angie was disappointed by her first day, I quickly changed the subject.

'Where's Brigit?' I asked. 'Haven't seen her for days.'

Fiona explained that she was staying at the hotel where she works, something about having extra shifts.

'She must have 1,000s stashed away in the bank,' Angie remarked.

'And the rest,' Rick added.

Suddenly the door burst open and Judith came running into the room. She pulled her backpack out and crammed something into it, before ducking into the bathroom returning with shampoo, conditioner and towel in hand. Stuffing these into her knapsack she waved good-bye and bolted out the door, slamming it shut as she went.

'Well, the smell's gotten to her too,' Rick said. 'Do you think she's told the manager?'

This morning, the stench in the room was sickening. It had now reached as far as the chest of drawers and seemed to be spreading by the second.

Leaving The Elms, I noticed a *Do Not Disturb* sign on the office door. I thought Judith or even Fiona must have complained about the smell. On second thoughts, Larry might have barricaded himself in there having tired of the sight of his own room.

Arriving at The Gazebo I found it hard to believe that I wouldn't be coming here for the next two weeks. I didn't know how I was going to fill my days and it saddened me that I wouldn't be seeing Jane, Chef or Gino during that time. I had become quite close to them all in the past weeks and, with Ron being away, I'd actually enjoyed coming to work.

Walking into the kitchen, I saw an agitated Chef frantically rewriting menus.

'What are you doing?' I enquired, wondering why he was choosing the last day of business to come up with new dishes.

'We have to use all the perishables. I have to redo the menus to minimise the waste,' he replied, without looking up.

By his gruff manner, I thought it best to leave him alone. Jane suddenly entered the room.

'Last day, can't wait. We're off first thing tomorrow. I'm really looking forward to this break.' Glancing across at Chef, she changed the subject: 'I wouldn't be a chef for the world. You think Gino could have mentioned this earlier.'

Chef looked up and smiled at her.

'It makes sense to use the stuff,' Chef remarked, casually shrugging his shoulders. 'No use complaining.'

Gino came in and washed his hands under the tap.

'I've been clearing out the office for the painters. I don't know where all the junk comes from. We need storage cupboards. I'll make sure they fit them when they're renovating.' Joining us for a cup of coffee, he looked over at Chef still busily scribbling away. 'Sorry about the last-minute changes,' Gino added. 'I didn't think of it until this morning.'

'It's almost there,' Chef said. 'But there will be some wastage. We have over 60 pounds of potatoes and I won't be able to use them all. I've included Shepherd's Pie, Latkes, jacket potatoes, as well as chips with just about everything except the sweets.'

'Well, stack all the produce you cannot use,' Gino said, 'and I'll get those miners collecting in Queensway to come and help themselves. Rather it feed the hungry than go in the bin.'

The day passed by remarkably quickly and despite the last-minute menu changes, we managed to serve the bustling Friday diners with surprising ease. Everyone seemed happy now about the enforced break. Even Gino talked about taking his family to the seaside. It was the first time I've ever heard him speak of his wife or kids. Jane and Chef were playfully affectionate with each other. As for me, I didn't really know how I'd fill in the time, thinking that perhaps I'd visit some of the sights.

After the lunch crowd had died down, Gino appeared with a group of miners. He had Chef serve them meals to ensure there were no leftovers. They then took whatever produce remained. As soon as we had tidied the restaurant, we all enjoyed a glass of wine, before locking up and going our separate ways.

Jane offered to drive me home, but I was really looking forward to the walk tonight. The air was warm, there wasn't much of a breeze and I knew there would be plenty of people out and about.

Arriving at The Elms, I felt refreshed and not at all sleepy. I noticed the sign was still in place on the office door and there weren't many people hanging around. In fact, I saw none of the familiar faces, not even Busman.

Opening the door to the room, I was bombarded by Angie and Fiona.

'Sit down, sit down,' they said in unison.

'Have we got news for you,' continued Fiona.

'What?' I said, momentarily oblivious to the disgusting stench in the room but a second later it hit me. 'Oh, that smell is revolting,' I frowned, as I sat down on my bunk.

'Forget that,' Angie remarked. 'Did you hear what happened last night?'

'Judith rushed into the room in a real state…' Fiona said.

'Yes, I was here,' I replied, wondering why they were telling me about it again.

'Well, she cleaned out the office,' Angie explained.

I suddenly had visions of Judith dusting the desk or stacking the sheets.

'She robbed the place,' Fiona added. 'Can you believe that?'

'She robbed the office?' I repeated. 'Really? What did she take?'

'Thousands of pounds, that's what,' Angie responded. 'Apparently there was a stash of rent payments in there, that were going to be deposited in the bank today. She cleared it out last night. That's why she was in such a hurry.'

'She picked the lock,' Fiona remarked, almost admiringly.

'The lock to the door?'

'And to the safety deposit box,' Angie added. 'A real professional, they say.'

'Who says?'

'The police, they were here,' Angie continued. 'They wanted to speak to residents, find out if anyone knew anything but as soon as the word got out, the place was empty. Everyone had disappeared. They couldn't even find Busman to speak to him.'

'I reckon if they checked this place out, they'd find a few wanted persons,' Fiona added. 'I've never known people to move so fast. One minute the lounge and the hallway are full with all the regulars and next it's like a morgue.'

'Did you speak to the police?' I asked, looking at them both.

'No way,' Angie replied. 'I don't want to get involved. It's none of my business. I'm just grateful she didn't steal from us while she was staying here. She could've quite easily. There was plenty of opportunity.'

'Yes, you have to respect her for that,' Fiona added. 'She turned out to be quite a good friend really. She could've taken the money from my wallet, but she didn't.'

I could see that in Angie's and Fiona's eyes, Judith should be canonised. After the initial excitement of recounting the saga subsided, I quickly changed the subject.

'Did you speak with the manager about the smell?' I asked Fiona.

'No, he wasn't seeing anyone today for any reason.'

'Well, we'll have to talk with him about it tomorrow. It's making my stomach churn.'

'You're not the only one,' Angie remarked. 'Rick can't come in here without retching. I'm sleeping with him in his room tonight.'

An hour or so later, Angie disappeared with Rick into the next room, leaving Fiona and I to suffer.

‘It’s like living in a sewer,’ I said, after unsuccessfully turning my thoughts to other things. ‘Do you think Angie would mind if I slept in her bed? I’m going to vomit. The smell seems to be worse, the closer you get to the floor.’

‘No, go ahead,’ Fiona answered. ‘Maybe it’s not in the wall, maybe it’s under the carpet.’

‘It could be,’ I replied, climbing into Angie’s bunk. ‘But to tell you the truth, I don’t know where it’s coming from any more. It seems to be everywhere.’

‘I think it’s under the carpet, under your bed,’ Fiona continued. ‘That’s where it started.’

‘Yes, you’re right,’ I answered, thinking back. ‘I first noticed it when I pulled out my suitcase. I couldn’t smell it anywhere else then.’

‘It’s under the carpet all right. I’ll tell them downstairs tomorrow.’

15 July 1984

There is an odour emitting from one of the doe cages. While it has not been confirmed, I suspect that it is urine. Both bucks and does mark their territory for many reasons.

Usually does mark at four-day intervals, just before they go on heat, to promote themselves to potential mates. Their urine profiles their sex, age, social status, even their level of fertility, among so many other details. A colleague once likened it to a lonely heart's advertisement which is a novel analogy.

Does will also mark if they need to be comforted. The smell of their own urine provides a sense of familiarity and makes them feel more at one with their surrounds.

Does may mark any new objects they come across, to denote their liking of the item or their ownership of it. They may even mark an object that has been moved.

Further to these explanations, marking may occur if a newcomer of either sex arrives. In this instance, the marking of urine by the doe is done to stake their claim, if you like, and denote their authority.

Bucks tend to do more marking than does. They do this to establish their dominance. In this way, bucks will not only mark territory but even subservient males. Bucks will also mark if they smell a female.

It is even common for bucks and does to urinate on the opposite sex. This is done for procreation purposes, a way of promoting their availability for mating when the time comes.

Over and above all these reasons, both does and bucks mark to find their way around. In this respect, their urine works in the same way as signposts.

Whatever the reason for marking, it tends to be more frequent where there are higher levels of testosterone. As such, fertile bucks mark more than neutered ones.

The doe cage in question is being frequented by a buck that has been temporarily neutered by injection. Though, in recent times, there has also been the presence of a wild rat. While it would seem more likely that the intruding rattus rattus is responsible for the odour, this buck has not been seen in the cage often enough for the excess of urine we are smelling.

As there is no obvious cause for the odour, developments in this cage will be monitored closely.

At the same time, I am noting increased hoarding among the subjects and even stealing. This is yet another indication that the increase in population, brought about by adding another subject to some of the cages, is already having an adverse effect.

Chapter 8

As I awoke this morning, I quickly covered my nose and mouth. My stomach began churning with the sickly stench, my mouth was rapidly filling with saliva and suddenly I felt hot and sweaty. Jumping out of bed, I ran for the toilet thinking I'd vomit at any moment. However, it was just a false alarm. Bending over the toilet bowl, I made up my mind then and there to have a shower and get out as quickly as possible. In all it took me about 10 minutes before I was on my way down to breakfast. The dining room was practically deserted and the kitchen was about to close. Grabbing the last piece of toast and a warm cup of tea, I sat at an empty table and, for the first time in a long while, ate on my own.

I needed to do some washing. But the thought of returning to the room to organise my laundry was too disgusting to contemplate.

'Anyway,' I thought, 'I have all of next week to wash clothes. It will give me something to do during my time off.'

After breakfast, I checked to see if the manger was in. He wasn't so, instead of hanging around and waiting, I walked down to Gloucester Road. Outside it was refreshing, even with the exhaust fumes. I took deep breaths to clear my lungs and hoped that my clothes weren't smelly after being in the stinking room. Gloucester Road was bustling, as the locals came out to do their weekend shopping. I walked up and down the street, looking in store windows, browsing through a few shops, making the odd small purchase; like air freshener, shampoo and the morning newspaper, then sat at the window table of a small cafe to watch the people pass by. My coffee was soon served and I opened the paper, glancing at the headlines: *Unemployment soars. Striking miners arrested.* Then, lower down the page, a pregnant Princess Diana could be seen visiting a hospice. Suddenly I heard someone knocking and, looking up from my newspaper, saw Michael smiling at me through the window.

‘You look very civilised sitting there with your paper,’ he remarked, as he entered the cafe. I could have easily taken offence to that comment, but instead let it slide. ‘Do you mind if I join you?’ he asked, taking a seat before I had a chance to answer. ‘I thought I might have seen you at the laundromat, just dropped off some clothes.’

‘No, I’m going to do mine during the week,’ I answered, taking a sip of my coffee.

‘I say that sometimes but then you get caught up with work and you never find the time.’

‘Oh, well I’m off for two weeks so that won’t be a problem.’

‘You’re on holidays?’

‘Well sort of, a forced holiday. They’re renovating The Gazebo.’

‘Going away?’

‘No, just going to hang around London. Maybe do some tourist things.’

The waitress came over and Michael ordered a coffee for himself, as well as another one for me. I felt that I should tell Michael about the stench in the room, in case he could smell it on my clothes. But somehow, I didn’t want to make The Elms seem any worse than he already thought it was.

‘I’m off to Greece next week. Corfu,’ he remarked. ‘A five-day shoot.’

‘Sounds good.’

‘Would you like to come along?’ I didn’t need to answer, the horrified look on my face said it all. ‘No, I mean as a friend. We can go as friends. You won’t need to pay for accommodation. Just your air fare and I can probably wangle that as well. What do you think?’ I casually shook my head. ‘Why not? You’re off work. It’s only for five days. You’ll love it.’ I shook my head again. ‘Well think about it. Don’t give me an answer now. Think about it, okay?’

Having finished our third coffees, Michael suggested we go back to his place for lunch. If it hadn’t been for the stench in my room, I would have declined. Walking to the mews with Michael I began to have second thoughts. Though, as it turned out, Michael was easier to be around than I had expected.

After preparing a salad, he opened a bottle of wine. Relaxing in his courtyard, eating and drinking, we had a pleasant time in each other’s company. By late afternoon, Michael was talking about us seeing a movie or something that night. However, I suggested another time would be better, making up an excuse to leave. At the door he asked me to think about accompanying him to Greece and

I promised I would. There was no awkward attempt at a hug as I left and I was relieved. Instead, we merely waved as I turned away to walk back to The Elms.

Climbing the seemingly endless flights of stairs to my room, I dreaded the thought of sleeping in my bed. The stench had been so overpowering the night before.

'Maybe I should change the bed linen,' I thought.

Entering the room, I noticed that no one was around, not surprising considering the odour that now greeted you at the door. Pulling my duvet from the bed, I managed to eventually remove the cover. It was times like this you noticed how cramped the room really was. Next, I took off the pillow slips and finally tackled the bottom sheet. At that moment Fiona walked in.

'Oh, poo,' she said. 'It's shocking. I couldn't talk to the manager this morning. He had some detectives with him,' she added, watching me struggle with the bottom sheet. 'This stuff reeks,' she remarked, referring to the linen piled on the floor. 'Any wonder you couldn't sleep in your bed.'

'I think you're right. It must be the carpet,' I added. 'That's why I'm changing the linen. The smell seems to permeate everything, even my clothes.'

'Listen, why don't you air your mattress out in the corridor while you fetch some clean sheets?' Fiona suggested. 'Ten minutes out there might help a bit.'

I agreed.

Pushing the linen on the floor aside to give myself some space, I went to lift the mattress while Fiona rushed to open the door. Grabbing the mattress, I swung it off the bed and then proceeded to stand it up in the tight gap between me and my bunk, before dragging it along the floor. Once I'd manoeuvred it into the hallway, I pushed my weight fully onto it until it was resting against the wall.

'What's that?' Fiona asked curiously.

'What?' I replied, pulling myself away from the heavy mattress to have a look.

'Those white things,' Fiona stated, pointing.

At first, I couldn't see what Fiona was pointing at but then I noticed them. These tiny, white beetle-like creatures were moving over the mattress base. There were so many of them, they seemed to merge with the pattern of the fabric. I stood back, clasping my mouth in horror.

'They're maggots,' I said, suddenly overcome with nausea.

'Maggots? On your mattress? No, couldn't be.'

Without waiting to answer Fiona, I ran back into the room, stumbled over the linen sprawled on the floor and stared at the base of my bed. Someone had laid white butchers' paper over the springs and there, on top, were layers of rotting red meat. The meat, now a dark brown colour, was covered in dried blood and home to hundreds of white crawling creatures.

'Ugh,' I screamed, retching on the spot.

'Oh hell,' Fiona added, as she stood beside me, covering her mouth and turning away. Hastily, I clambered over the discarded duvet to the bathroom and vomited into the toilet bowl. With clammy hands and sweat covering my brow, I vomited again then wiped my mouth with some tissues. 'Are you all right?' Fiona asked, appearing at the doorway.

I nodded, waving for her to leave, before I vomited again. Fiona waited outside the door as I continued to be sick into the toilet bowl. No matter how many times I threw up, the uncontrollable nausea kept returning in waves until there was nothing left to expel except fluid.

Finally, I managed to stand and, wetting a towel, washed my face before running the cloth over my throat and around the back of my neck. Cupping my hands I filled them with cold water from the tap, swished it around my mouth then spat it out. I repeated this a few times until the vile taste had disappeared. Eventually I emerged from the bathroom.

Fiona had begun to wrap the rotting meat in the butchers' paper and I helped her complete the task. Then, carrying the foul parcels downstairs, we headed straight for the manager's office. He was on the phone and brushed us off with his hand, so Fiona dumped the meat parcels on his desk stopping to scribble a message on the paper.

'What did you write?' I asked Fiona, as we returned to our room.

'I just said that someone had planted this under your mattress. Then I added no prizes for guessing who.'

'You think it was Brigit?' I enquired.

'Well, I can't think of anyone else. Can you?'

Back in the room I grabbed the linen on the floor and took it downstairs to the office. The manager wasn't in there, nor the meat parcels. I assumed he was disposing them. I gathered a clean quilt cover, pillow slips and sheet before returning upstairs.

Fiona was in the process of making Brigit's bed when I walked into the room.

'What are you doing?' I asked.

'I've just swapped your mattress with hers. She won't know. They're exactly the same.' I sprayed my bed base with air freshener and then pulled the bed out to spray the carpet underneath. Placing the mattress on top of the springs, I proceeded to make the bed, before pushing it back against the wall. Fiona grabbed the pot plant, that usually stood on the chest of drawers, and used this to keep the door to the room open. 'Get some air in here, eh?' she said, and I agreed.

While she was doing that, I tried to open the window but it wouldn't budge. Fiona, seeing me struggle, used her weight to give it an almighty shove and soon fresh air poured into the room. Well, as much fresh air as you can expect with all the diesel fumes. In the midst of this cleaning, Angie and Rick returned.

'Smells like a bed of roses in here,' Angie commented.

'It's that,' Fiona explained, pointing to the container of air freshener sitting on the chest of drawers. 'Brigit put rotting meat under Elizabeth's mattress,' she added. 'That was the smell.'

'Rotting meat,' Rick repeated.

'Yes, it was covered in maggots,' Fiona continued. 'Revolting. Made Elizabeth throw up.'

'Well, it explains why she's not been here,' Angie remarked.

Fiona and I nodded.

Brigit didn't return that night, not that I really wanted to see her. To be honest, I didn't know how I'd react if I was confronted with her smug face. No, it would be better for both of us if she stayed away. That night I felt an incredible loneliness. Not that Angie, Rick and Fiona didn't include me in the conversation, they did. But there was a feeling of alienation. Brigit could have had a vendetta against any of us. We had all upset her from time to time. It wasn't difficult to upset Brigit. Sometimes, you only had to breathe to make her seethe to the point where the vein in her forehead protruded. Yet it was me that she hated. As I lay in bed that night trying to get some sleep, I knew it was not over with Brigit. She would do something else and I would have to be more vigilant.

Sunday morning, I awoke early. I hadn't slept well, tossing and turning all night then waking in a cold sweat. It seemed from one o'clock onwards I had opened my eyes at 10-minute intervals, so I was less than refreshed when I stumbled out of bed. Angie and Rick were asleep in the top bunk, their bodies wrapped around each other. Fiona was lying spreadeagled on her bed, muttering in her sleep.

After showering and dressing, I wandered downstairs for breakfast. Sipping tea, my thoughts kept returning to Brigit. Whether she was here or not, it didn't matter. You felt her presence regardless. If it wasn't for Brigit, I would probably be content to stay at The Elms for some time. However, now I didn't know how I would get through the next week, let alone the months ahead.

Having placed my breakfast dishes on the trestle table, I walked out of The Elms. I didn't really know where I was going, that didn't seem important. I just needed to get away for a while and gather my thoughts. Subconsciously, my feet took me down the street that led to Michael's house.

As I walked along, I stopped at the narrow lane where he lived, then made my way to his door. I didn't know the time. I'd left my watch back in the room, so I knocked regardless. After my second attempt, I heard his groggy voice coming from the upstairs room overlooking the lane way.

'Coming,' he yelled.

He was bare-chested, and in the process of tying his sweatpants, when he opened the door. He seemed startled to see me.

'When do we leave for Greece?' I asked.

'You're coming?'

'If I'm still welcome.'

'Sure. That's great. Wednesday,' he replied, smiling.

'Okay, I'll catch up with you later to talk about the arrangements. You know, what flight I should book.'

'We can talk about it now, over a cup of coffee,' he suggested.

'No, I need to walk. Later, okay?'

22 July 1984

Unusual behaviour has been noted in one of the doe cages. The does appear to have scraped the newspaper from the floor of the cage and dragged this into the connecting tunnel.

Upon closer examination the newspaper was very damp but it is highly uncommon for rats to clean their hutch, burrow or, in this case, cage. I have never witnessed rats doing this and, after further investigation, I have found no evidence anywhere of this having occurred before. While rats, of both sexes, will groom themselves frequently throughout the day, they do not "clean house".

It is imperative that newspaper, or any material they use for bedding, is kept dry. Otherwise, rats can suffer respiratory ailments and skin infections, among other health issues. I admit that I had not inspected the cage closely enough to notice the wet paper. It was well under the top layer. Even so, I am at a loss as to why the does removed this paper themselves.

One explanation could be that rats would normally move away if their living quarters became damp. However, in the study, they do not really have the ability to sleep elsewhere. The other cages are full and there is not enough room in the communal areas with others coming and going all the time.

Of course, another explanation could be that it has nothing to do with cleaning. For instance, it could be an attempt to stop other rats from entering because their cage is attracting outsiders and becoming cramped.

Either way, this development has been highlighted as a behavioural change that can be attributed to population increase.

Chapter 9

For the next few days I was distracted, preparing for my trip to Greece. Michael offered to organise my air tickets and accommodation but I still had to buy a few things and sort out storage for my belongings. Given recent events, I didn't want to leave my possessions lying around. I still had not seen Brigit since discovering the rotting meat and I didn't want to have to deal with her until I returned from Greece. Hopefully she would stay away a couple of days longer.

Monday morning, Larry emerged from his self-imposed solitary confinement. However, he was still very subdued, preferring his own company.

'What's up with Larry now?' I asked Tom, over breakfast.

'He's getting over his mood. He'll be right in a while. Best left alone when he's like this.'

'Good morning, Elizabeth.' I looked up to see Busman, with his cup of hot tea, preparing to join us.

'Hi, how are you? I haven't seen you around.'

'Oh, there were detectives in and out of the place last week. I had a bad experience with the legal system once. I prefer to lie low these days.'

'Yes, apparently someone ransacked the office,' Tom added, 'stole a stash of rental payments.'

'Well, I didn't see anything so it was no use me speaking to any detectives,' Busman commented, taking a sip.

'The model is almost completed,' Tom announced, biting into his piece of toast.

'We worked on it all last week,' Busman remarked. 'It's a beauty all right.'

'Should be finished by Friday,' Tom added. 'I think your friend will be right pleased. It looks like something you'd buy from Christies, an heirloom of sorts.'

'Well, I'm going to Greece for a holiday so I'll have to see it when I get back. I can't wait. It sounds wonderful.'

'Greece? I could tell you a few tales about the islands,' Tom remarked.

‘How long are you going for?’ Busman asked.

‘Only five days but it’ll be a nice change.’

‘That it will,’ Tom nodded. ‘We had a fella on board, Pete was his name. Well on one of our trips to Greece, he skipped ship and never returned. You know when you serve in the navy, you’re not supposed to do that. It’s desertion. But he didn’t care. He loved the place with a passion.’

Later that day, I spoke with the manager. He was very apologetic about the rotting meat episode, saying he’d take it up with Brigit on her return. I told him to leave it, explaining that his intervention would only make matters worse. After mentioning my trip to Greece, he suggested putting my belongings in the storeroom downstairs. We arranged for me to bring down my case on Wednesday morning, just before I left for the airport.

Returning to the room, I gave Angie a phone message that she was required for two classes tomorrow. She seemed less than eager, and I wondered if she’d still be working as a life model when I returned.

‘Who’s in the bathroom?’ I asked. ‘Is Brigit back?’

‘No, a new roommate, Simone, she’s from Belgium.’

Suddenly the door opened and a girl appeared with ghostly white, facial powder, red lipstick and black geometrics drawn from her eyes to her temples.

‘Hi,’ she said, acknowledging me standing there.

‘Hi,’ I replied. ‘I’m Elizabeth.’

She smiled and, collecting a towel from her allocated bunk, disappeared back into the bathroom.

Monday evening, I went through my clothes and selected what I would take to Greece. Angie and Rick were smoking a joint in the top bunk, Simone had gone out and, strangely, Fiona hadn’t returned from work. Come midnight I crawled under the covers of my bed and, listening to Rick’s rhythmic snoring, eventually fell asleep.

I awoke quite late this morning, almost missed breakfast. The dining room was practically empty. Timothy sat at one table sorting through a pile of papers. I glanced his way to see him glaring at the kitchen hand and muttering something to himself about “Pakies”. Perhaps Fiona was right about his fascist leanings. With breakfast out of the way, I headed down to the tube.

Arriving at Oxford Street, I became lost in the crowds that seemed to push me along with my feet barely touching the ground. I located the swimwear section in one of the department stores and proceeded to sort through the rows of lycra. I eventually decided on a plain black bikini and, after quickly trying it on, parted with 30 pounds and left.

Next stop was the pharmacy where I bought sun screen, a hat, shampoo, conditioner, as well as some travel sickness pills, just in case.

I called into the bank and changed my pounds into traveller's cheques, then sat down in a cafe for a coffee and pastry, before making my way back to The Elms.

Arriving in the room, Simone was painting her nails. We smiled at each other, before I deposited my bags on the bed and left to phone Michael.

'Everything ready for tomorrow?' he asked. 'We leave 11.30am from Gatwick.'

'Yes, that's fine. What time should I get to your place?'

'Just before eight. Now I've got your tickets. This travel agent owed me for some shots I'd taken in Portugal, so they're on the house. Accommodation is arranged and I've got plenty of film. You won't need a camera.' I felt a little uneasy about my travel being free. 'You still there?' he enquired.

'Yes, but I can pay for the tickets and the hotel,' I replied.

'No need to. They didn't cost me anything.'

I spent the rest of Tuesday packing my overnight bag. I figured lightweight clothes would be all I'd need, with the remainder of my belongings squeezed into the suitcase, ready for storage.

Tuesday night and still no sign of Fiona. I began to worry if she was all right.

'Have you seen Fi?' Angie asked, returning from work.

'No, I was just thinking about her,' I answered, eating my yoghurt and fruit.

'Two nights in a row, not like her to stay out.'

I nodded.

'How was your day, better?' I asked.

'Yes, I'm getting used to this statue stuff, I think. They were friendlier this time, more talkative, a different crowd.'

'They're not the same students then?'

'No, they come from art schools all over London. This lot was more fun, less serious. Some of them showed me their work after we'd finished. You know I'm no art critic, but none of their sketches looked like me at all. Sometimes my face was this blank oval shape and in others I was quite angular.'

'So do you think you'll stick it out?'

'Oh, I don't know, early days, but the extra cash is good.'

‘Well, I’m ready,’ I stated, putting my suitcase over by the wall next to my overnight bag.

‘It’ll be strange you not being here, what with Fiona gone too?’

‘Oh, I’ll be back next week,’ I added. ‘You won’t even know I’ve gone.’

I went to bed not long after, worrying that I wouldn’t wake up on time if I didn’t get an early night. Angie assured me she would be up at seven, because she had a morning class, and that she’d wake me first thing. I seemed to lie awake for hours possibly out of anxiety or excitement, maybe a combination of both.

Eventually Simone returned to the room and we chatted for a while. Then Rick turned up and told us he’d heard from his lawyer. She was optimistic that the court hearing would be within the next month.

‘You should just leave it,’ Angie said, her abrupt tone indicating her annoyance.

‘I can’t leave it. They’re my kids. As much mine as they’re Kate’s.’

‘But you’re not going to get visitation rights and then you’ll be devastated. Honestly, I don’t know why you put yourself through this time and again.’

Rick ignored Angie’s remarks and proceeded to undress for bed. Angie sighed and, by the way the springs creaked, I gathered she’d rolled over to face the wall. Rick, standing there in his jocks, looked at me and shrugged before getting a footing on the window sill and hoisting himself up.

This morning, I arrived at Michael’s house with my overnight bag filled to bursting. He was busy organising his camera equipment into two metallic cases. He folded down a tripod and then, wrapping his rolls of film in foil, proceeded to pack them into his bag.

‘The cab is on its way. Do you want a cup of coffee? The pot’s still warm.’

I walked into the kitchen and poured myself a cup but, as there was no milk, I tipped it down the sink.

‘Cab’s here,’ I heard Michael call and, bundling our baggage out the door, we set off for the airport.

What with checking in our luggage and locating the appropriate gate, Michael and I didn’t stop until we were settled into our seats and on our way. It was a turbulent flight, probably because we were travelling in one of those lightweight planes. So, I declined all offers of food or drink and instead tried to catch up on some of the sleep I’d lost the night before.

29 July 1984

Having audited all cages and interconnecting tunnels, it appears that another two does have gone missing. One is the largest of the rattus norvegicus does. She has not gone missing before so I am checking all cages. The other is a doe that has not been seen for an extended period of time so it became imperative to replace her.

The new subject has unusual markings. If it were possible, she could be taken for a cross between a rattus rattus and a rattus norvegicus domestica. However, this is unlikely. The rattus rattus and rattus norvegicus are different species. While coupling may occur if they are kept in close confines, there have been few reported incidences of fertilisation resulting from this pairing. When it does, miscarriage follows. There is just one documented case of a rattus rattus and rattus norvegicus producing a living litter but they did not survive.

More cages have been added. This time, the new subjects were not slow in venturing into the tunnels. In fact, they actually converged on one of the communal cages with such force that the other subjects went into hiding. In particular, the older rats seemed quite scared of the newcomers and stayed out of their way. Since then, the new subjects have settled and are no longer drawing attention.

Chapter 10

The road meandered its way around a cliff face. On one side, were rugged slabs of stone, relieved only by the occasional plant growing against the odds. On the other side, the edge of the bitumen bordered a sheer drop to a sea of crystal clear, azure waters. Eventually the curves and bends led us to five, small, pastel-coloured buildings, surrounded by sea views.

'This is Paleokastritsa,' Michael announced. 'There's a monastery up on that hill.'

I looked around. It seemed very quiet, almost remote, with only one person to be seen, walking on the beach. Michael paid the cab driver before removing our luggage. As the road went no further, the cab driver did a U-turn and continued back along the winding road to Corfu Town.

The Lazarus Hotel stood before us; a small, three-storey establishment painted pale yellow. At ground level, a veranda with tables and chairs led to a tiny office. The attendant told us our rooms were on the first floor so, with keys in hand, we scaled the stairs.

Michael opened the door to my room and I placed my overnight bag on the chair. The room was clean but spartan, thc only othcr furniturc being a small table, double bed and wardrobe. I was pleased to see it had its own bathroom. With whitewashed walls, white linen and simple pine furniture, it was clear that no colour was required, not with the impressive panorama, spanning the bluer than blue sea and lush, green landscape.

Michael's room was next door, so having arranged to meet in 15 minutes we both went to freshen up.

'I've just checked, the hire car's parked downstairs. Want to come with me to Corfu Town and look over the clothes I'll be shooting tomorrow?' The hire car turned out to be a Fiat 126; a small, white vehicle that made Michael seem enormous by comparison. 'It always takes me a day or so to get used to driving on the right,' he admitted, as we careered around the first bend. I secured my seat belt.

'So, what are you shooting here, clothes?' I enquired, once we were on a straight stretch.

'No actually mopeds. This new range of cheap bikes called Fast Legs.'

'Fast Legs,' I repeated.

'Yes, so they're using leggy models, skimpy clothes. You know, very original,' he added, with a hint of sarcasm. 'Anyway, we're just shooting at sunrise and sunset, so we'll have lots of time for sightseeing.'

Arriving in Corfu Town, we were greeted with columned, stone buildings encasing a square. There were holiday-makers everywhere, shopping or queuing to ride on the brightly painted carriages, lined up like a wagon train. Michael parked the car and then, ducking through a lane way, we arrived at a bevy of restaurants. He quickly scanned the tourists, dining at tables on the pavement, before waving to a woman seated on her own.

'That's Penny,' he announced, grabbing my arm to cross the road.

'Penny?'

'The stylist,' Michael explained. Penny smiled as we neared her table.

'So much for punctuality,' she remarked. 'I've had four gorgeous fellas try to pick me up. But I turned them down because of you. Hope you feel bad.'

'Not really,' Michael shrugged. 'Penny, this is Elizabeth.'

'Hi,' she said, looking me up and down. 'It's about time you gave those bimbo models a miss,' she added, and I didn't know whether to feel flattered or offended. 'Can I get you two coffees?' Penny asked. 'I'm just about to order another.'

'I'll get them,' Michael offered.

'No, I will. The waiter is really cute,' she smiled, before grabbing her wallet and disappearing inside.

'Penny's great. I use her on most jobs. Been working with her for years,' Michael commented.

When Penny reappeared, the conversation turned to business. Penny had Polaroids of the clothes she'd selected. Michael agreed with her choices. Next, they looked at photographs of the talent; four models in all. Michael perused the shots and helped Penny organise a call sheet. Looking at her closely, I assumed Penny was in her early-30s. Her love of bright colours obvious in her vivid clothing and also the unnaturally, red hair that framed her face. With her playful personality and ready laughter, I found her easy company on this sunny afternoon.

After an hour or so of discussions, Penny went to phone the talent and confirm the shoot times. Upon returning, she assured Michael that everything was set. The make-up artist, the models and the mopeds were expected at five the next morning, as well as an assistant they'd both worked with before. Michael asked Penny to join us for dinner but she declined, saying she had some last-minute details to sort out.

Come nightfall, Michael and I were seated in the pebbled courtyard of a clifftop restaurant. Michael ordered a jug of Retsina and dips for starters.

'I'm glad you came,' Michael said, as we sipped wine. 'I really am sorry about what happened.'

'You don't have to keep explaining. That's already been settled.'

'But it's changed things? To you I'm some kind of tosser?' Playfully I pretended to think and then nodded in agreeance. 'Well don't hold back,' he laughed. 'No need to worry about my feelings.'

After a nightcap of Ouzo on the veranda, Michael and I eventually parted ways. The long day had caught up with me and I was feeling exhausted. But, for some reason or another, I just couldn't sleep. I tried lying on my right side and then my left. I took one arm out from under the covers and then two. I gave the foetal position a go and, when that didn't work, I stretched out flat. I stuck one foot out from under the sheet and then my entire leg. I remembered reading somewhere that if you slowed your breathing, sleep soon followed. Still, no matter what I did, I was wide awake.

I wondered how Angie and Rick were doing, mentally visualising them squeezed into the top bunk. I worried if Fiona was all right, trying to picture Julian as something other than an opportunistic old boy. I also pondered peculiar Brigit, imagining her all-familiar smirk when she hears I've gone away. I realised then why I couldn't get to sleep. It was the first time in ages that I'd had a room to myself.

Michael was already at work when I awoke this morning and, looking out from my window, I decided on a swim. A fisherman unloading his catch rubbed his arms, and pretended to shiver, to warn me that the water was cold. Ignoring his advice I ran and dived under the first wave, re-emerging a short distance from shore.

‘This water is nothing compared to the shower at The Elms,’ I thought, as I floated on the undulating surface, allowing the waves to bring me back into the shallows.

After my dip, I lay outstretched on the towel, the sun soaking up the moisture. It was delightfully warm on the beach. A gentle breeze seemed to hover just above my body and lulled me into a semi-conscious state. I was only vaguely aware of the sound of the waves and the occasional sea bird calling. I could have stayed there all day but, as I’d arranged to meet Michael, decided to make a move before I fell into a deep sleep.

Sometime later I was showered and dressed. Michael was already an hour late and I was now wet with sweat, from sitting under the veranda’s tin roof with its unrelenting, radiant heat.

‘I’ll give him a little while longer,’ I thought, wiping my forehead with a tissue. Suddenly the attendant at the office, hurried over with a phone message that Michael was delayed. After my initial annoyance, I opted for a walk up to the monastery to fill in some time.

The climb up the winding hillside track seemed to lead me into the heavens, my expectation increasing as the calf muscles in my legs ached, then groaned and eventually cried out in agony. Around the next bend, I was relieved to finally be standing on flat ground. In front of me was a series of stone arches, an insignificant belfry and a simple single-storey building, which I discovered was out of bounds.

Other than a few chickens pecking at the ground, I wandered around alone. Approaching a stone ledge, I looked out over the expanse of Mediterranean Sea glistening below, telling myself the view was well worth the steep ascent. Muscle sore and weary, I eventually arrived back at the hotel to see Michael sitting on the veranda enjoying a beer.

For the next few hours we lunched, then inspected the local wares.

The nearby open-air market was in reality a dozen or so card tables, erected under the shade of the olive trees that lined the roadside.

Browsing through the assortment of hand crafts, I chose six woollen sweaters with Angie, Rick, Fiona, Tom, Busman and Larry in mind. They were thick and well made, just the thing for the harsh London winter ahead. Surprisingly they were also very cheap.

‘You wear a lot of sweaters?’ Michael asked, eyeing my purchases.

‘No, they’re for my friends at The Elms,’ I explained, and he didn’t comment further.

That afternoon, when Michael returned to the shoot, I wandered down to the beach on the far side of Paleokastritsa and perused the rocky shoreline. Since arriving in Greece, I’d felt a little out of sorts, unusually edgy and at the same time despondent. I’d put it down to anxiety, thinking that deep down I really regretted coming here with Michael. After all, it was pointless spending so much time in his company when nothing could or would transpire.

I strolled the water’s edge leaving temporary footprints in the sand, imagining Tom in a naval uniform staring back at me through binoculars. Recalling his anecdotes, I visualised his crew mates, the banter, the laughter and the heavy drinking sessions at each port of call. It was a far cry from how he spent his days now. Looking down, I noticed a very shiny shell with quite unusual markings. Picking it up, I held it to my ear, the air in the canal mimicking the sound of the ocean. Brushing off the sand, I popped it into my bag and continued on my way.

When I arrived back at The Lazarus, Michael was parking the car.

He waved.

‘We’ll eat across the road and then head out. Penny might meet us at Soula’s later on.’

‘Soula’s?’

‘It’s a club. She’s managed to score a date with some waiter.’

Later that evening, the drive along the winding coastal road had me on tenterhooks. I knew that Michael’s judgement might not be up to par, having finished off a bottle of wine over dinner. With no street lighting, and a road that twisted and turned, I had visions of this vehicle lying at the foot of a craggy decline, deluged by waves. However, my fears were unfounded. In fact, the drive to Corfu Town was relatively trouble-free, compared to the next 30 minutes or so we spent trying to find a car park.

Having eventually scored a spot many blocks away, Michael and I then stumbled along uneven paths, in the direction of the music.

With the patrons spilling onto the street, it was difficult to get inside the door but, after a little pushing, we managed to make our way through the crowd. Michael said something to me but I couldn’t hear him, what with the club-goers’ raised voices and techno beat of the bass reverberating off every surface. So, instead, he pointed. There was a woman staggering from the dance floor towards us, her arms outstretched. Screaming with exaggerated excitement, she reached for his face with both hands then planted a kiss on his lips.

'Come on, let's have a dance,' she suggested, grabbing Michael's arm and dragging him into the sea of bodies.

Michael turned back and indicated for me to wait as he tried to unleash himself from her grip. But instead, he was pulled further into the dance floor, until I could only see the occasional glimpse of the top of his head. Suddenly someone was tapping me on the shoulder. It was Penny.

'Where's Michael?' she mouthed. I pointed towards the dance floor. Penny then asked another question but I couldn't make out the words so, taking my hand, she led me into the bathroom. 'What's Tanya doing here?' she said, as soon as we were on the other side of the door.

'I don't know. She just turned up.'

'Turned up? She stalks him.' She paused for me to comment but when I didn't, she continued. 'I can't stand the woman,' Penny added, taking the opportunity to retouch her make-up.

'Why?'

'She's trouble. A total drama queen. I've worked with her on shoots. When he told me they'd split up, I couldn't have been happier. He's such a good person, he deserves so much better. But she's a nightmare, a recurring one at that.'

Penny licked her teeth to clear them of any lipstick before checking her smile in the mirror. Having popped her make-up back into her purse, she started adjusting her bra, pushing her breasts upwards and then together, before standing back to admire her now over-the-top cleavage.

'Well, it must be okay with him or he wouldn't put up with it,' I suggested, trying to hide the fact that Tanya was now bothering me as well.

'No, she's got the whole damsel in distress thing down pat. Always going on about this fellow called Alastair. Truth is he is just a ploy to make Michael jealous.'

Emerging from the ladies' room', we ran into Michael who was looking for us in the crowd. The music had momentarily ceased, so at least we could speak.

'Tanya's here,' he announced, as if we didn't already know. Penny and I stared at him. 'She's had a fight with that cock she's been seeing. Needed to get away.' Penny and I stared. 'She wants to join us?' Penny and I stared. 'You okay with that?' he asked and, not waiting for an answer, went to get Tanya while Penny and I found a table.

‘She didn’t look too damned upset to me,’ Penny commented, as she slid across the seat in a corner booth that had just been vacated. Her words were cut short by the appearance of Michael, with Tanya draped over his body like a trench coat.

‘Just one more dance, oh come on, please,’ Tanya oozed, desperately trying to drag him away.

‘No, really, I’m bushed,’ he answered curtly. ‘This is Elizabeth,’ he added, ‘and of course you know Penny.’

‘Regrettably,’ Penny muttered.

‘Oh, come on. Just one more dance,’ Tanya pleaded, grabbing his hand with both of hers.

‘No, honestly, I want to sit this one out,’ Michael stated, pulling his arm away. Tanya stumbled a few steps backwards then proceeded to dance solo. ‘You want to get going?’ Michael said, turning his attention to me. ‘It’s getting late.’

‘What and leave Penny?’ I asked.

‘No, I’ll be right. I’m with George. He’ll be back in a moment. Just go.’

She seemed very keen for us to leave while Tanya was distracted and I was happy to oblige.

5 August 1984

Does keep disappearing from the same cage. Having just replaced one doe, the runt also appeared to be missing and the one named "Australia" was nowhere to be seen as well.

This morning, upon closer inspection, I located the runt in one of the connecting tunnels. But there is still no sign of "Australia". This subject has repeatedly been seen with a wild rattus rattus and returned. So, I will not replace this doe for a week, just to be sure.

Of course, it is concerning that so many rats keep escaping. The recent territorial markings could be impacting rats in that cage. I have documented that the rats removed the newspaper as this was an indication of their dislike for the scent.

Their leaving could also show their unrest and this has been duly noted. However, they could not go missing unless there was a flaw in the colony structure. So, the behaviour of escaping may be because of the scent, or merely due to these rats being opportunists and taking advantage of an opening they have found.

Either way, I will be closely monitoring the occupants of that cage in the days ahead.

Chapter 11

The drive back was quiet. Michael seemed a little distracted and I was too tired for small talk. But as we saw the faint lights of Paleokastritsa in the distance, Michael suddenly spoke.

'Want to sleep in my room tonight?' he asked, his eyes fixed firmly on the road ahead. I hesitated, a little taken aback. 'It doesn't have to be anything sexual. I just want to hold you, be close to you,' he continued. It was a line that I'd heard before. Every woman has. But maybe this time it was true.

No sooner had we unlocked the door than Michael made a beeline for the bathroom. Standing there, staring down at his double bed, I wondered why I'd agreed in the first place. I heard the toilet flush and a few minutes later Michael was back, now busying himself with setting the alarm. I went to the bathroom, hoping that when I reappeared Michael would be in bed, but he wasn't. Instead, he was still fully dressed, this time, fiddling with his camera equipment.

I had the impression that Michael was waiting for me to decide the dress code. As Michael was seemingly fascinated by his camera case, I took the opportunity to unzip my dress and slip it down over my hips. As I stepped out of the fabric, now bunched around my feet, I also discarded my shoes. I paused a little unsure but then unclipped my bra, only leaving on my briefs. Picking up the abandoned clothes I draped them over the wooden seat then, lifting the covers, slid my body under the sheet.

Michael quickly put his photographic equipment away and then proceeded to undress himself, down to his jocks. Climbing into bed, he threw one of his pillows on the floor and plumped the other into shape before switching off the light.

For a moment or two we both remained on our sides of the bed. Then turning towards each other, Michael stretched out his arm as I curled up alongside his body, resting against his bare skin. The next few seconds were spent getting comfortable. I gently eased my thigh over Michael's as he opened his legs to accommodate our now entwined limbs. With my head nestled just beneath Michael's chin, I could clearly hear his heart beat. I stroked his chest with my fingertip while he, in turn, ran his hand up and down my back. For a long time, it seemed, we lay there just like that.

I don't remember feeling drowsy but suddenly I was awakened by the alarm clock. Michael reached over and switched it off, then rolling back, wrapped his arms around me. Pulling my body into his, he kissed me on the lips, first teasingly and somewhat cautiously then deeply and with more feeling. The next hour passed by in what seemed like minutes and now Michael was late.

As I remained in bed, Michael hurriedly showered and dressed, kissing me again before leaving. As soon as the door banged shut, I went back to sleep, totally spent from my late night and early morning.

Most of the day had passed, when I eventually dragged my body out of bed. I'd missed breakfast and lunch. However, the restaurant opposite offered to make me a Greek Salad, even though the kitchen was closed. As I sat there nibbling tomato and feta cheese, I thought about Michael. I was in two minds about what had happened. Not that I regretted it, I didn't, but there was something inside telling me not to get involved. Looking at my watch, I wondered why Michael was so late returning. He should have been back hours ago and I hoped there hadn't been any dramas at the shoot. By evening there was still no word from Michael.

'Must have decided to hang around Corfu Town,' I thought.

I couldn't blame him; it was unbearably hot today and the Fiat had no air conditioning. Even I didn't want to venture too far, preferring to stay in what little shade I could find, reading my book.

Come nightfall, I was getting hungry and, after grabbing my bag, decided to dine alone.

It was almost midnight when I left the restaurant. Walking back, I couldn't see the Fiat and was suddenly concerned that Michael may have had an accident. My fears were unfounded. As I walked towards the stairs, the hotel attendant handed me a note from Penny. Michael had asked her to let me know that he'd be late back. Apart from my initial annoyance, I wasn't too perturbed and just continued onto my room.

Sometime later, I heard someone hammering, but in my semi-conscious state pulled the covers over my head and drifted back to sleep. I heard the noise again, though it wasn't hammering, someone was knocking on the door. I sat up and, for a moment, looked around the room startled. Then I remembered I was in Greece. It was morning. Jumping up, I concealed my body with the sheet before opening the door. Michael was standing there, red-eyed and unshaven.

'What time is it?' I asked.

'It's almost nine. I just got back,' Michael answered, walking in and plonking himself down on the crumpled bed, before running his hands through his hair. 'I've been up all night,' he explained. 'Tanya was threatening to kill herself because she's broken up with that prick.' By the look on my face Michael could see that this conversation was not going any further. 'But Tanya's not your problem,' he said, acknowledging my silent protest, 'and she's not my problem either.'

It was early afternoon before Michael and I emerged from the room, freshly showered, dressed and packed. We were checking out. Now that Michael had finished shooting there was nothing to keep us in Paleokastritsa.

As we approached Corfu Town it was bedlam. Cars appeared out of nowhere and disappeared just as swiftly, the only evidence of their exit being a cloud of dust that floated for a few seconds then settled. In the town, buses tooting their horns caused havoc as they hustled for more space on the one lane streets. Pedestrians strolled nonchalantly on roadways only moving marginally, after much coaxing, to allow us to drive through.

Signs seemed non-existent and when visible were confusing. Reversing out from one dead-end after another only added to our mounting tension. Symbols appeared on just about every street we attempted to drive down indicating *no entry*, *one-way traffic only*, *no left turn*, *no right turn* and all the time people obstructing our every movement. When we finally left Corfu Town, we were stressed to the limit and looking forward to an early night in much quieter surrounds.

The road took us to Dassia, and we checked into the first hotel we saw. It was quaint, obviously a family business as a young boy took down our details. Michael was now feeling the effects of his sleepless night and yawned repeatedly through dinner. By nine we were in bed and despite our weariness managed to find some energy, before falling asleep in each other's arms.

The morning sun streaming into our room woke us and, after a filling breakfast, we checked out and ventured on our way. For the next few hours, we drove along the coastline with a tranquil sea view heightening our sense of wellbeing. Cruising along, I looked over at Michael. His eyes were no longer red and his face was free of stress lines making him appear almost boyish.

Turns eventually took us inland as arteries of dirt and crushed stone led us to crusty villages, as vague as the inhabitants who sat and stared as we invaded their turf. Unshaven men with weather-beaten faces seemed lost in their thoughts, while their wives waited in anticipation for a stranger to direct. Donkeys carried the elderly women, their teeth missing, their sagging breasts barren and their grey hair in scarves to protect it from the dust. Being a person who lives for imagery, Michael was in his element.

By nightfall, Michael and I secured a small shack overlooking the sea, with stone walls and floor, along with shuttered windows.

Sitting on a picnic rug, under the clear, star-filled sky we feasted on olives, cheese, flat bread and wine we bought in the last village. With a gentle breeze to keep the heat at bay it seemed silly to sleep indoors. So, eventually we grabbed two pillows, along with a sheet and camped out.

Next morning, as soon as we had washed and dressed, we loaded the car and set off once again. It was our last day in Greece and we didn't want to waste a minute. We drove along the coastal road for as long as we could before turning inland.

'I'll be sorry to leave here,' Michael commented, over dinner. 'I've become used to having you around.'

'Well, I'll be around, just in the next street.'

'Or you could move in?'

'What? As in live together?' I asked.

'Yes. What do you think?' I paused for a moment or two, wondering how to decline without hurting his feelings. 'You can't stay at The Elms forever. You have to find somewhere to live,' he continued, sensing my reluctance.

'But you shouldn't just live with someone…'

'No, I suppose not,' he snapped, before I'd finished what I was saying and, turning to the waiter, asked for the bill. The atmosphere was a little strained as we drove to the last hotel and when it was time for bed, we went straight to sleep. When Michael's alarm sounded, he was already in the shower, so I used the opportunity to pack the rest of my things.

'Good morning,' Michael said, finally emerging from a cloud of steam. 'The bathroom is all yours.'

No sooner had I dressed than we were downstairs, checking out.

Little more was said on the way to the airport. Michael informed me that he'd called the car rental firm giving them details of where they could collect the Fiat. Apart from that, he kept his eyes on the road and I watched the passing view from my window.

12 August 1984

It has been a major exercise but all subjects have been removed and counted. Then once emptied, each cage has been inspected for any gaps large enough for rats to escape. A rat requires a 20mm opening. Even so, to allow for the smallest runt in the colony, I checked for any holes measuring half that size.

Every wire was stress-tested also. In particular, I was looking for any give, the kind of flexibility that would allow the rats to push the wires apart. Finally, I checked all tunnels, paying particular attention to where they joined the cages. Yet, for this intensive and time-consuming investigation, no flaws whatsoever were discovered in the colony structure.

This leaves me with only one logical conclusion as to how rats are coming and going. My experiment is being sabotaged.

In the days ahead, I will put together a list of everyone who has access to the laboratory. I will also be monitoring their movements; the times they visit, the duration, as well as the reason. I will then match this data to any subject that vanishes or indeed reappears.

It is regrettable that valuable laboratory time is being wasted in this way. However, we must be certain that controls are not being compromised by foul play. After all, my entire work's creditability is now at stake.

Chapter 12

As soon as we were seated, Michael told the driver: 'Remington Road, South Kensington.'

The trip back was amicable with just enough small talk to take the chill from the air. As we pulled up outside The Elms Michael helped me remove my luggage, then kissed me on the cheek before resuming the last leg. Once the cab had turned into the next street, I looked at The Elms, remembering the first time I stood here with luggage in hand.

'You're back. Good trip?'

I turned to see Busman carrying out his ever-vigilant London Transport surveillance work.

'Yes, wonderful,' I said, giving him a hug.

'Well, you must come up and see the model. It's finished. She's exquisite, even if I say so myself.'

Inside, I saw some of the old faces. I nodded at Larry, sitting in the hallway, and he gave me just the hint of a smile, before looking down to remove some imaginary fluff on his sleeve. Timothy was reading and looked up as I passed.

'You again?' he said. 'I thought you must have left.'

'No, just been away a few days.'

'Elizabeth!' Suddenly Tom came bounding towards me. 'Elizabeth,' he repeated, 'do you want to see the model? It's finished. She's a real beauty.'

'I'd love to, as soon as I put my things away.'

'Room 89 in half an hour?'

'Make it an hour,' I suggested.

'An hour it is,' he smiled, grasping my hand. 'Good to see you, can't wait to hear all about Greece. Bet you had a fabulous time.'

'Yes, I did. I'll fill you in on the details later.'

Making my way into the office, I interrupted the manager who was busy sorting through some paperwork.

'Welcome back,' he said, peering over a pile of what appeared to be bills.

'Thanks, can I get my things now, or would you prefer I come back later?'

'No, now's fine, here's the key. The storage room is just around the other side of the stairs.'

Grabbing my suitcase from the suffocating camphor-scented room, I returned the key before tackling the stairs with my lumbering baggage. It was a struggle to climb the three flights, what with a heavy suitcase, overnighter, as well as a plastic carry bag containing six weighty sweaters and a shell. By the time I reached the door to the room, my pulse rate was racing with the strain.

Unlocking and pushing the door open with my case, I was confronted with the sight of Brigit, lying back on her bed, reading a magazine. By the look on her face, she was displeased to see me. Leaving the case, I carried in my overnight bag and the sweaters, throwing them on my bunk. Returning to the door, I now dragged in my final piece of baggage, before pushing it out of the way beneath the bed.

Brigit sighed and said something under her breath but I pretended not to notice, preferring to ignore her obvious contempt for me. Simone was sitting on her bunk, painting her nails in glossy black varnish. We smiled at each other.

'Did you have a nice time?' she asked, in her heavily-accented English.

'Yes thanks. Anything happen while I've been away?' She shook her head. 'Is Fiona back?' I asked, looking at her bed.

'Yes, she is at work.'

'Oh good,' I replied, relieved to hear that she was okay.

Pulling my overnight bag from the bed, I proceeded to empty the contents and sort the dirty clothes into piles. Brigit sighed again, this time a long deep moan that lasted a few seconds. Picking up my haircare bottles, I walked to the bathroom to place them by the shower. As I emerged, Brigit sat up.

'You know you are really starting to bug me,' she snarled, with her top lip curled. I stopped momentarily to reply but instead opted to walk away. 'Did you hear me?' she asked, as I knelt on the floor, sitting on my legs.

I ignored her again but perhaps I'd pulled a face or rolled my eyes. I must have done something because of what happened next. From my seated position, I suddenly saw Brigit leap from the bed. Before I could move, she was lunging at me, slapping me across the face with her magazine; once, twice, three times, until I managed to snatch it from her hand and toss it across the room.

With the full force of her weight, she body slammed me backwards, her digging claws clasping at my throat as I gasped for breath. I was desperately trying to unleash her hold over my now restricted airways but, as my legs were pinned down under the weight of both our bodies, I was stuck. As she squeezed at my throat with an ever-tightening grip, I was convinced my face must be turning blue.

Grabbing at her arms, her shoulders, her hands proved pointless so, feeling I was about to lose consciousness, I reached for her hair and yanked it. Her hold loosened momentarily as I screamed 'get off'. But just as soon as the words were out, her fingers clenched at my throat with such a force, I knew she was intending to kill me. In sheer panic, I gained strength from somewhere and with all the might I could muster, heaved her to one side. Her body toppled from my torso and jumping up, I prepared to kick should she come at me again. 'I could have you for assault,' I retorted, rubbing my burning throat.

'I hate you, you fucking bitch. I want you gone. You fucking hear me,' she screamed, spit shooting from her bared teeth.

I could have snapped back, almost did. But instead opted for silence. Not a silence that is derived from having nothing to say or being scared to speak up. I just knew that my voice would tremble and that would be seen as a sign of weakness. I had to appear unfazed even though my heart was pounding. I could not give her the upper hand and so I didn't. When Brigit did not get the reaction she wanted, she slowly stood, straightened her skirt, collected her magazine and returned to her bed.

Looking across I saw Simone, still sitting on her bunk. She raised her eyebrows. Summoning as much composure as I could, I calmly returned to sorting through the remainder of my laundry. With that out of the way, I ventured downstairs to pick up some clean linen. While I was in the office, I complained to the manager who was still pre-occupied with his paperwork. Without looking up, he offered to move me to another room.

'No, I'll stay where I am,' I answered, defiantly. 'I refuse to be bullied.'

Lifting his head, he suddenly noticed the red welts around my throat. Taking a closer look, he promised she'd be evicted as soon as her next rental payment was due.

'She's probably paid six months in advance,' I thought, but thanked him for the gesture regardless.

With fresh linen in hand, I entered the room again. Brigit grinned as I walked past her bed.

I ignored her. As I set about tucking in the sheet, I could sense she wanted a response from me, a verbal rebuke. I had done nothing to Brigit to warrant her contempt and now this violent outburst. I knew she wanted to somehow justify her actions but I wouldn't participate. I wasn't going to allow her the opportunity to substantiate her repeatedly vicious behaviour.

A short time later, as I was walking to Tom's room, I burst into tears, a delayed reaction no doubt. After taking a few minutes to dry my eyes, I continued on determined to enjoy the rest of the afternoon. Pulling my collar over the stinging flesh, I knocked on Tom's door.

'Hold on a tick,' he yelled. From the unexpected barrage of noise emitting from the room, it sounded like he'd decided to suddenly rearrange the furniture. 'Right, you can come in,' he called.

Opening the door I saw Tom, Busman and Larry standing side by side, concealing the model from view.

'Welcome Elizabeth,' Tom announced, as Larry and Busman smiled. 'We decided to have a little presentation. I hope you don't mind the formalities.' After taking my seat on Tom's bunk, he continued with the proceedings. 'Lady and Gentlemen, we are gathered here to officially unveil the latest addition to the Royal fleet; a fine, hand-crafted vessel that will hopefully surpass all expectations. Elizabeth, will you take the champagne?' Tom handed me an empty bottle, instructing me to hit the bed post and announce the vessel's name. I was a little uneasy about breaking glass in such a confined space but I didn't want to spoil the fun. 'Are you ready Elizabeth?'

I nodded.

We all watched as Tom pulled aside the pillow slip to reveal the galleon, under a glass cover. On the bow was scribed the name, *Elizabeth*. Standing with the champagne bottle poised I thought of some appropriate words.

'I hereby announce the maiden voyage of the Elizabeth, a fine galleon and the pride of any fleet.'

With that I smashed the bottle against the bedpost but nothing happened. I tried again, yet this time it only cracked. Eventually Larry snatched it from my hand, hitting the bedpost repeatedly until only the bottle neck remained.

'That's enough,' Tom remarked. 'Enough!' Quickly we took it from him before he could do any harm. 'So, what do you think?' Tom asked, placing the bottle remains in the bin.

'She's stunning,' I answered, truthfully. 'You should feel very proud of your workmanship,' I continued, addressing all three of my friends.

'Well really Tom did most of the work. We helped out now and then, but it was Tom who did all the tricky stuff,' Busman explained. 'So, do you think your friend will be pleased?'

'Oh, I think he'll be delighted. He was in the navy for many years you know and he misses the sea. This will make a nice keepsake don't you think? The romanticism of sea life captured forever.'

'You're talking about Tom?' Busman asked.

I nodded.

'You bought it for me? Oh, Elizabeth, this model must have cost you a fortune. It's one of those top-of-the-range ones. What can I say? Oh, Elizabeth, thank you from the bottom of my heart. I will treasure this gift forever.'

With the unveiling over, I handed Tom, Busman and Larry the sweaters I'd purchased in Greece, as well as the shell I'd found on the beach. Tom placed this alongside the galleon. The afternoon ended with a bottle of beer which we drank from foam cups, as I filled them in on my trip. We chatted and laughed for the next hour or so and, then, suddenly it dawned on me. For once Busman wasn't at all bothered about schedules or watching the time and that was really good to see.

I was dreading returning to my room, but I knew I couldn't delay the inevitable any longer. Sooner or later, I would have to see Brigit again.

'Anyway,' I thought, 'she'll be at work by now.'

Opening the door, I noticed Brigit was still reclined on her bed reading her magazine. She didn't look up. Angie smiled from her ever-familiar spot on the top bunk, Fiona acknowledged my entrance with a warm greeting, while Simone gave me a friendly nod.

'So how was it?' Angie asked. 'Can't wait to hear all the details.'

'Yes, tell us all the good bits,' Fiona added. 'Don't want to hear about a whole lot of stone statues.'

'Oh, I'll tell you later,' I explained, sitting on the bed to remove my shoes.

Even though I was trying hard to conceal my feelings, the strained expression on my face clearly indicated that all was not well. Fiona looked at me strangely.

‘What’s wrong?’ she whispered. ‘Are you okay?’ With tears welling in my eyes, I eased down the collar of my shirt to reveal my reddened throat. ‘He did that to you?’

‘What? What did he do?’ Angie asked, suddenly looking over the side of the bunk for a better view.

I waved at them to be quiet and pointed to Brigit who, thankfully, had her back turned to us.

‘She did that to you?’ Fiona mouthed. I nodded. Angie jumped down from the bunk and took a closer look, shaking her head as she carried out the inspection. ‘What happened?’ Fiona mouthed. I contemplated how I could recount the details without drawing Brigit’s attention and, after a moment’s consideration, reached for some paper.

After scribbling down a brief summary, I handed the paper to Fiona who looked over the words before passing it onto Angie. Fiona mouthed the word: “Bitch”, before settling back onto her bunk. Suddenly she grabbed the paper and, borrowing my pen, jotted down a reply: *Don’t worry, we’re here. I’d like to see her take us all on.*

Fiona’s support didn’t alleviate my concerns, nor soothe the scorching sensation I felt emitting from the flesh on my throat. Still, I appreciated her kindness.

I hadn’t yet looked at the damage and disappeared into the bathroom to do just that. Locking the door, I stared into the mirror. Across my neck were reddened lines of raised flesh. If it wasn’t for Brigit’s finger marks, you’d assume I’d been viciously scratched by a feral cat.

Surprisingly, Brigit did not venture out so, after accepting some fruit from Fiona, I sat on my bunk eating and pondering my future. Simone changed into something black and left for a night’s entertainment on Kings Road. She asked if any of us would like to come along and I was tempted to accept. However, after the day’s activities, I was simply too exhausted to wander anywhere. As Simone left, Rick arrived. Brigit by now had hopped into bed and, by her heavy breathing, seemed to be asleep. I took this opportunity to hand out the souvenir sweaters as Angie and Fiona, both whispering, filled him in on what had happened.

‘She’s a psycho, all right,’ he commented. ‘Why wasn’t she thrown out?’ I shook my head, explaining that her rent was paid in advance and nothing could be done until her next payment was due. ‘Then best stay out of her way,’ he advised, trying on his sweater and running his hands over the wool.

While I knew that Rick meant well, it was easier said than done.

‘I should’ve moved in with Michael,’ I thought, getting ready for bed.

19 August 1984

Play fighting is common among rat pups, adolescents and sometimes even young adults.

It may take the form of pinging, where they excitedly and harmlessly pounce onto each other then remove themselves just as quickly. This action may occur repeatedly and is often interspersed with bouts of running around the cage.

Another form of play is where one rat chases another. This tends to end amicably, with the pursued rat allowing the dominant one to groom him.

Even boxing can be a form of play that is often seen in burrows. Play fights tend to occur between young siblings and, in these cases, may even continue right through adulthood. In fact, play fights happen regularly and are part of normal everyday interaction.

At the same time, adult bucks are also known to fight but for more serious reasons. In these cases, it tends to be about establishing hierarchy or proving dominance. Interestingly, alpha bucks are not known to be aggressive, until they are targeted by upstarts. If the challenging rat submits, the fight tends to end before any real injury is inflicted. However, sometimes, these do turn into full blown battles of bared teeth, saliva and claws. While unpleasant to watch, these conflicts are to be expected in all rat colonies and, indeed, are essential to maintaining a degree of order.

What I observed today, however, was unusual. A deliberate display of aggression between does that was so extreme, it could have become a fight to the death.

From the onset, this was a typical instance of pouncing followed by pinning, a form of attack where one rat, using their body weight to hold down the other, then bites or claws. The attacking runt had fluffed fur and its tail was wagging. Both are signs of aggression. The victimised rat showed no desire to submit and, instead, fought her way free and prepared to kick, yet another way rats inflict harm.

The runt from this cage has increasingly been acting oddly. This rat has been remaining near the water bowl for longer periods. This could indicate that the rat is feeling more insecure. The rat in question also recently went missing for a lengthy period before being located, hiding out in a rarely used tunnel. Again, this could denote nervousness and perhaps fear. Both of which could have led to the unprompted attack.

The other rattus norvegicus also disappeared recently. So perhaps, as they had both been apart, they may not have recognised their scents and seen each other as threats.

Either way, as the colony population is continually growing through the addition of more cages, this has been noted as a behavioural change.

Chapter 13

Despite a restless sleep, I was relieved to still have a pulse. I'd half expected Brigit to suffocate me during the night. But thankfully that hadn't happened. Sitting up I noticed the culprit was already in the bathroom, her bed having been made and her black pumps neatly placed on the floor. Turning I saw Fiona yawning and rubbing her eyes.

'Where's the claw?' she asked, squinting to see without her spectacles.

'She's in the bathroom.'

'Oh, great,' she replied, falling back onto her pillow. 'I've already had two warnings for tardiness.'

'I have some talcum powder in my bag,' I said. 'Why not use that instead?'

'Rick not here?' Fiona asked Angie, standing and noticing that he wasn't in the top bunk.

'He slept in his room last night. He wanted to read some legal stuff he got from the library. You know how Brigit is about the light being on.'

'What legal stuff?' Fiona enquired, powdering her armpits.

'You know, family law. He's reading anything and everything he can find on the subject. At this rate, he'll get a legal degree without even trying.'

'Well good luck to him,' Fiona stated, checking her watch on the way out. 'You can't blame him for wanting to see his kids.'

As soon as the door slammed shut, Brigit returned, and sitting on her bed, slipped her feet into her shoes.

'Shouldn't she be at work?' I asked, after Brigit had exited the room.

'I think she's lost her job,' Angie remarked. 'She's here most of the time these days. Hardly ever goes out and if she does, it's only for an hour or so. Anyway, it probably doesn't matter. It's not like she's short of money. It's Fiona I'm worried about.'

'Why?' I asked, a little puzzled.

'Because of this Julian character.'

'You don't like him?'

'No, I don't even know him. But from the little she tells me; I think he's using her. You know he's married?' I nodded. 'And he's 50.' I nodded again. 'And his name's not really Julian.'

'It isn't?'

'No, Fiona told me she made that up because he's some big wig in politics.'

'Well, why tell you that in the first place?'

'She was stoned. She probably doesn't even remember mentioning it.'

I still had a few loads of washing to do and decided to tackle these domestic duties. The laundromat was busier than usual, perhaps because it was a weekday and people were now on their lunchbreaks. Standing in line I eventually passed over the bags of dirty clothes and, turning, saw Michael.

'Fancy a coffee?' he asked.

As all the cafes were filled with office workers, Michael suggested his place and grabbed my hand to cross the road. Even though few words were said, I could sense he was in a better mood than when I last saw him. As he unlocked the door, he suddenly noticed my throat.

'What's this?' he asked, running his finger down the length of one of the welts.

'Oh nothing,' I answered, trying to cover the marks with my hand.

'Doesn't look like nothing to me,' he replied. 'Was it a cat?' he enquired.

'You could say that,' I shrugged.

'They allow animals in the room?'

'No, I was being sarcastic. Brigit did it. You know, the one I said was strange.'

'What did she do?' he asked, shutting the door behind us.

'Oh, she sort of attacked me. My unpacking was apparently getting on her nerves.'

Michael's eye's widened as he inspected each wound more closely.

'That's not okay you know. Not okay at all. You have to get out of there.' As Michael filled the kettle with water, I browsed through the shots he'd taken in Greece. Ignoring my every effort to change the subject, Michael was now suggesting that I move in, even if I wanted to stay in the spare room. 'I'm not trying to pressure you,' he reassured me. 'I just don't like you living like that.'

We decided to forgo the coffee and spent the remainder of the afternoon in bed, with Michael repeatedly asking me to reconsider and me declining his persistent attempts. I knew that Michael couldn't understand why I wouldn't leave my cramped living conditions. In a way I didn't understand either.

It was evening before I walked back to The Elms, so distracted in my thoughts that I completely forgot about my laundry. Opening the door, I was greeted by the all-familiar sight of Brigit, lying on her bed. It was enough to make me take Michael up on his offer, but instead I asked Angie if she fancied going out.

'What you and me, to a restaurant?' she responded, temporarily taken aback. This was quickly followed by: 'Yes, why not?' now seemingly excited by the prospect.

Two hours later Angie, Simone and I were walking down Kings Road. At the entrance to the Beaufort Market, there was a cluster of leather jackets, *Support the miners* signs and fluoro mohawks. The dirty and somewhat dishevelled clothes hanging off the strikers' backs were oddly matched by the punks' safety-pinned, faux leather pants and calf-high combat boots. Together they mingled, carefully eyeing London's constabulary watching on from the other side of the road. At this point Simone saw her friends who were there to be pierced, tattooed, or have their hair spikes coated with egg whites and she left to join them.

'I never go out to dinner,' Angie commented, once we were seated in a pasta restaurant. 'But what the hell, eh?' After ordering our meals, we watched the passers-by, remarking on this one and that. An elderly lady reminded Angie of her gran. 'She thinks I work in an office you know. It's funny, I don't care about anyone's opinion, except hers. That's why I let her think I'm a secretary. So, she can feel proud when she tells her neighbours.'

'Has she met Rick?' I asked, wondering if their relationship had gone beyond the confines of The Elms.

'No, but she'd like him. She'd fatten him up too. Ordinarily I wouldn't have looked twice at someone all skin and bones like Rick. I usually go for those macho types. You know big and brawny. But we just sort of clicked right from the start,' Angie admitted, butting out her cigarette so the waitress could serve our risotto.

It was quite late by the time Angie and I entered the room at The Elms. Brigit was muttering in her sleep. I stopped to listen, just in case I heard my name mentioned, but I couldn't make any sense of what she way saying. Fiona's bed was empty. Simone's bunk as well, not that I had expected her to beat us home.

As I tried to fall asleep, I thought about Michael, Fiona's relationship with Julian and finally Ron from work, wondering when she'd return to The Gazebo.

'Why am I thinking about her?' I thought. 'Now I'm bound to have nightmares.'

Come morning, Angie surprised everyone by being the first in the shower. She had an early morning life modelling class. I could have quite easily stayed in my bunk, nestled under the covers. But as Fiona and Simone were still out, I didn't fancy the idea of spending my day alone with Brigit. I was convinced she'd planned her next attack and this made me uncomfortable in her company.

As soon as the bathroom was vacated, I took a shower and dressed, applying a little make-up to detract attention from my fatigued eyes and sallow complexion. That done, I picked up my bag and headed down to breakfast.

Shouts could be heard well before I reached the foyer and there, before me, was a line of diners backed all the way along the corridor. Tom waved for me to join him.

'Saved you a spot,' he said, pointing to the empty chair opposite. Pulling up a seat between Larry and Jasper, I was surprised to see they were sharing just two pieces of crust, that hadn't even been toasted. 'Kitchen's run out of bread this morning,' Tom explained, noticing me staring. 'That crowd there isn't too pleased. Been standing around for an hour. If they don't serve up food soon, I reckon there'll be a riot.'

Just then the staff brought out two loaves and the crowd converged on the trestle table.

'Move back,' called the kitchen hand, 'before someone gets hurt.' But rather than contain the queue, the group had closed in and were now threatening to storm the pantry.

'If you're going to take in more residents, you need to tell catering,' Tom stated, careful to move the plate of crusts closer to the centre. 'For most of the people here, this is their only feed.'

'Stand back. Stand back,' the kitchen hand shouted, but there was no stopping the hungry hoard. As jostling for position erupted into punches, chaos ensued with the staff soon overpowered.

'You not working these days?' Tom asked, pitching his voice against the argy-bargy that was fast becoming an all-out battle.

Just then there was an almighty crash. The trestle table had collapsed along with its crockery contents. Momentarily distracted, we turned our heads to the source of the noise. Then resumed our conversation.

'No, they're renovating the restaurant. Didn't I tell you?' I yelled in reply, wondering to myself if perhaps we should sit somewhere safer.

'You might have,' Tom answered, seemingly happy to stay put.

'They're painting, recarpeting and getting new furniture,' I explained, loudly emphasising each word to be heard over the kerfuffle. 'I start back next week.'

'This place could do with a bit of work,' Tom shouted, as a chair was thrown through the window, the entire leadlight panel shattered, a glass slither flying towards us and landing just shy of his tea cup. 'Behind my dresser the other day I found a newspaper. You know what was on the front page?' he continued, his elbows now resting on the table as he leant forward to tell us. 'Di's and Charles's wedding,' he laughed. 'That's how long it's been since they've cleaned behind there.'

'Who are Di and Charles?' Larry asked, now also moving his seat closer.

'Prince Charles and his wife,' Tom elaborated, brushing the last piece of crust to rid it of any glass particles.

'Did Prince Charles get married?' Larry enquired, taken aback as Tom nodded. 'Well, they certainly kept that quiet.'

Angie had finished her class by the time I returned to the room. She was being openly affectionate with Rick, sharing her cigarette, stroking the stubble on his chin and listening to his every word, completely immersed in his company. It was times like this that I truly believed they were made for each other.

By nightfall, Fiona had still not returned. These days we'd all noticed she'd been staying away more frequently. As Rick climbed into Angie's bunk, he jokingly made some comment about Fiona's whereabouts. But despite playing it down, I could see that he too was a little concerned about her extended absence.

Come morning I considered calling into the club where she worked but thought again. While we had become quite close, Fiona was still very much a private person and I suspected she would not welcome me turning up. After all, she had gone to great pains to keep Julian's real identity quiet. That's the thing about sharing a room. With so much exposed, on show, in full view all the time, it really is quite remarkable how little we know about each other. As if boundaries have to be in place, to help maintain a little distance, we create our walls with bricks of withheld information.

With Angie working longer hours, even Rick was keeping to himself more these days. Most of the time he was in his room next door, only turning up in ours after dark. In fact, until my enforced break from The Gazebo, I hadn't realised how often they were apart now. But given their volatile relationship, perhaps it would do them both good.

Walking into the dining room this morning, I was surprised to see the shattered window had already been boarded up, the trestle table erected and the crockery restacked. Though I was hard pressed to find a plate and mug without a crack or chip.

Tom, perusing a diagram of sorts, made room for my tea and double serving of toast as I joined him at the table. He explained that he was starting on his next model, having purchased one himself, then proceeded to show me the complex instructions.

'When I finish this one, I'm going to have a go at designing a model myself. Jasper has offered to help me. With all this time away from the mine, he's really missing working with his hands.'

No sooner had he gone than Rick sat down.

'Sleep well?' he asked, stirring his tea cup endlessly until I was sure he'd score his way through the porcelain.

'No, I was tossing and turning.'

'You and me both,' he remarked, taking a sip before stirring again. 'Angie's making a fair quid out of this life modelling,' he said, helping himself to my now cold toast. 'I've never seen her happier. It doesn't stop her complaining, of course, but that's just Angie. For her to be up and dressed before sunrise, she must be getting something out of it.'

Suddenly on breakfast TV, there was a breaking news report about the spread of HIV. Instantly, scarf-wearing Timothy jumped to his feet and turning, addressed the room.

'That's right,' he nodded. 'It's the plague of today sent to cleanse our society. Let's hope it kills off all the pervs and then spreads to the Pakies.'

26 August 1984

Ordinarily, all test subjects are euthanised after each experiment. This is done with carbon dioxide, by decapitation or through injection, whichever is deemed the most pain-free and humane at the time. However, for this study, we are using subjects that have been involved in other tests.

As it was imperative to mirror a society it was crucial to have subjects of various ages, experiences, some that were strangers, as well as rats that were already familiar with each other.

Increasing each cage by one subject is progressing well and about half way through. At the same time, additional cages have been linked to the colony, allowing for even more occupants.

In line with population growth, we are seeing repeated incidents of hissing and huffing. Not just from the bucks but also the does. It appears that aggression can now simply be triggered by rats sharing space, though food is also becoming an issue.

This week grain containers were filled in the communal eating cage. But before seed could be mixed in, the rats had converged on the supply in an almost frenzied manner. It's as if they are becoming fearful of a shortage of grain as the colony population grows. It's the same with the water and we are noting that subjects are drinking from the supply in their cages more often.

Attacks are also on the increase. Given the issues we are seeing with food, I wonder if they could possibly resort to cannibalism if their sustenance appears to be compromised. Being omnivores, this behaviour would not normally be associated with rats, but given recent developments it's not entirely out of the question.

Chapter 14

After spending Saturday and Sunday night with Michael I was in desperate need of a long, uninterrupted sleep. With that in mind, I'd ventured back to The Elms last night. On my arrival there was still no sign of Fiona. Her bed untouched, except for a small indent where Simone had stepped to climb up to her bunk.

This morning as I willed myself to kick off the covers, I looked around. Brigit was still asleep, the same Cleopatra position, hands crossed neatly over her chest. Simone was snoring, her loose arm hanging over the edge. And by the huge lump in the mattress above, Angie and Rick were also dead to the world.

'Just my luck,' I thought. 'When I want to sleep in, everyone's up and when I can't stay in bed, they're all comatose.'

I took my time in the bathroom. For once the shower was piping hot and I stayed under its spray for as long as it took to stir my drowsy senses. With no one to interrupt me I was soon dressed, hair styled and make-up in place, ready for my return to The Gazebo.

The dining room was much quieter than usual, most people having already eaten. With no queue to join, I walked straight up to the trestle table and helped myself to tea and toast.

I was looking forward to seeing Jane, Chef and Gino. I wasn't sure if Ron would be back, so there was no point worrying about her at this stage.

The exterior of The Gazebo had been totally revamped. The interior too was hardly recognisable.

'What do you think?' Gino asked.

'It's made a difference,' I said. 'Much better.'

'I'll take you on a guided tour,' he suggested, playfully offering me his arm.

Suddenly the cloakroom door burst open.

'Well don't just stand there Elizabeth. We have guests coming for the opening party,' Ron snapped. 'There's a lot to be done.'

‘Not until I show Elizabeth around,’ Gino interrupted, nodding for me to take his arm.

‘Why?’ Ron snarled. ‘She’s got eyes in her head. She can look all she wants after closing.’

‘No,’ Gino emphasised. ‘I wish to show Elizabeth the renovations and I will do so before outsiders. Is that clear?’ With that Ron frowned and, turning on her heel, headed for the kitchen. ‘That woman’s only been back a few hours and already my blood pressure’s sky high,’ Gino remarked, shaking his head.

For the next 10 minutes Gino showed me every change they’d made, even down to the door handles. He seemed immensely proud of the renovations, taking full credit for every decision, including the new logo on the menus which I knew had been the work of a graphic designer. Still, his ever-flowing enthusiasm was refreshing and a welcome contrast to Ron’s persistent pessimism.

‘Elizabeth!’

As my name was screamed from the kitchen, I cut short my conversation with Gino and obediently reported for duty.

On the bench were a pile of napkins which Ron wanted folded into flower shapes. Even though it took Ron five minutes to demonstrate how to fold one napkin into this intricate pattern, I was expected to do over 100 in less than half an hour. I tried to explain that this many napkins couldn’t be folded in so little time, but Ron wouldn’t listen. In the midst of my frantic handiwork Chef entered the kitchen, his arms laden with platters.

‘Would you believe they’ve invited over 100 guests for this opening party and what notice have we been given?’ I could tell by Chef’s flushed face and flamboyant gestures that he was about to go into one of his tantrums. ‘Food critics from every leading publishing house and what preparation time have I had?’

‘You’re back,’ I heard and, turning, saw Jane’s smiling face at the doorway. ‘It’s so good to see you,’ she said, giving me a warm hug. ‘I had this awful feeling that you wouldn’t front up today and what with this damned party…’

‘Yes, I was just telling her all about it. I’ve a good mind to walk out.’

‘You and me both. Have you seen Ron yet? She’s certainly got her broom out today.’

I nodded not wanting to stop working on the napkins. I’d only done 10 and there were 90 to go.

'Jane, oh there you are,' Ron interrupted, sighing. 'Have you finished polishing the new silverware because there's a list of things to be done?'

'It didn't need polishing, it's new, just needed a wipe over.'

'No,' Ron disagreed, 'the silverware has to be properly cleaned, every last piece.'

'Then you do it Ron, I have tables to set.'

With that Jane exited the kitchen much to Ron's aggravation.

'If she's not careful, she'll be out of here before the day's finished.'

'Is that right?' Chef remarked. 'Well, if Jane goes, I follow. And without me, all your precious guests go hungry.'

'It's just that we have an awful lot to do,' Ron continued, trying to placate Chef.

'Yes, and I have a hell of a lot more to do than you. So, get out of my kitchen and let me get on with it.'

With that Ron turned and left the room.

'Where are the table cloths?' Jane asked, wandering back in.

'Did you look in those new storage cupboards? The ones near the office.'

'Didn't know there were any.'

'Jane, if I see you in here once more…' Ron scolded, waltzing through the doors.

'You'll what?' Jane retaliated, leaving in search of the cupboards.

Obviously, Jane managed to locate the cloths and the tables were draped in linen.

'Elizabeth, the name tags,' Ron exclaimed, handing me a tray of cards each inscribed with a guest's details. I looked at them blankly. 'For the table next to the entrance. Lay them out in alphabetical order. It will make it easier. Well, go on,' she ordered, dismissing me with her hand. Having delegated all tasks, Ron disappeared leaving Jane, Gino and I to carry out the last-minute preparations. She returned sometime later wearing a cocktail dress of all things, her transformation rendering us speechless. 'Do I look the part?' she asked, slowly turning to give Gino full view of the backless number.

'The part of what?' Gino asked, still taken aback.

'The part of the hostess of course,' she giggled, before going into the kitchen to check on Chef's progress.

'How long has Ron known about this party?' I asked, thinking that she must have had the gown especially made.

‘Oh, she helped me send out the invitations last week,’ Gino explained. ‘She’s certainly gone to a lot of trouble,’ he added, shaking his head in disbelief.

The first to arrive was the proprietor, Charles Potter, along with his PR machine. His greying hair and excessively lined face were belied by a boisterous, energetic manner. He enthusiastically greeted Gino with a heavy-handed pat on the back, before turning to address me.

‘Charles Potter,’ he said, holding out his hand to shake mine.

‘Elizabeth Pearce,’ I replied, as his firm grip nearly crushed my bones.

‘Well, you’re doing a wonderful job there Elizabeth, keep up the good work.’

One by one everyone was introduced, as his team of PR consultants and photographers wandered around viewing the renovations.

‘He’s a friendly fellow,’ Jane remarked, coming up to help me, ‘and rolling in money. That’s why I think Ron’s gone to so much trouble.’

Shortly afterwards the guests began arriving. Ron, still chatting with Mr Potter, seemed oblivious to the fact that her assistance was required. I busily handed out name cards, while Jane carried around a tray of champagne, mineral water and chilled fruit punch. Even Gino assisted, weaving through the ever-growing crowd with platters of mouth-watering canapes. Thankfully Mr Potter was keen to mingle, extend his business contacts and, in the nicest possible way, managed to unleash himself from Ron.

‘Tanya Philips,’ I heard and, turning, was confronted with Michael’s ex, standing there with a smirk on her face. ‘Oh, you’re a waitress,’ she oozed, with exaggerated fascination.

Handing over her name tag I quickly turned my attention to the next guest in line, as Tanya wandered off to greet someone.

Whoever calculated that 100 would be attending had obviously overlooked the onslaught of journalists. Eavesdropping on some of the guests, I learned that Potter is a big-league operator in the corporate world, constantly making headlines in the financial press for his unorthodox business acumen. By the influx of reporters, even a restaurant refurbishment is an event if Charles Potter is the proprietor.

An hour or so later, when most of the name cards had been issued, Ron took over at the entrance telling me I was needed on the floor.

Perusing the room, I noticed Jane carrying two platters and Gino handing out drinks, each run off their feet by the seemingly never-ending demand. Walking to the kitchen, I armed myself with platters before becoming lost in the room full of revellers.

'Another glass of champagne.' Looking up, I saw it was Tanya who was making the request.

'The drink waiter will be over shortly,' I answered, struggling to unchain my overburdened tray from someone's shoulder bag.

'Oh, you can get it,' she waved, forcing her empty champagne flute into my face. 'Better make that two,' she added, dropping it onto my platter of miniature smoked salmon crepes.

'What's this?' Chef asked, removing the glass. 'Next, they'll be butting out their cigarettes in the food. Fancy a coffee?' he asked.

'No, I have to get back.'

'One cup won't hurt. That lot can wait. They haven't stopped eating since they arrived,' he remarked, handing me the piping hot beverage.

'Thanks,' I replied, taking a sip, happy to relieve the weight from my bruised and aching feet.

Outside the hubbub became hushed as Potter, speaking through a microphone, greeted his guests. From the kitchen we could hear his confident voice booming, probably because I'd left the door ajar. His light-hearted manner was appreciated by intermittent bursts of laughter from the crowd. At the end of his speech, applause rang out before he was barraged by the hoard of journalists about some pending take-over bid.

Come late afternoon most of the guests had departed, leaving only a small gathering of sloshed journalists and press photographers standing around. Ron was thoroughly enjoying herself in their company as Jane, Gino and I busily cleared away the vast quantity of glasses, dishes and ash trays, before removing the cloths and wiping down tables. Gino called to order pizzas and suggested we sit down as soon as the food arrives. After ushering the last of the journos out the door, Gino returned to join us.

By midnight we were still talking and laughing about the day's activities. Ron was not impressed by our camaraderie and suggested more than once that we should be cleaning the toilets. Gino was about to explain that he had hired a cleaner, but his sentence was cut short by someone knocking on the door. Ron, standing and straightening her dress, tottered off to see who it was. She returned with her arm around Michael's waist, mistaking him for one of the men she'd spoken with earlier.

'Would you like a drink?' she asked, pointing to the collection of champagne and beer bottles on the table.

'Yes, a beer would be great,' Michael answered, smiling at me.

'Have you met my friends?' I asked, not remembering if I had formally introduced them. 'Michael this is Jane, Albert, Gino and Ron.'

'And what do you do Michael?' Gino asked.

'I'm a commercial photographer,' he replied. 'Thanks,' he said to Ron, who after providing the beer was trying to nestle her way in between the two men.

'Interesting work?' Gino continued, leaning forward to see around Ron.

'Can be, depending on what you're shooting. There's a lot of location work involved, a lot of travel and that's an added bonus. Elizabeth and I were in Greece last week to take some shots of a new range of mopeds. The actual shoot wasn't too interesting, but it's always good to get away.'

'You didn't tell me you were in Greece,' Jane accused, playfully poking my arm.

Ron gave me a darting glare.

'Well, we were so busy today. Didn't get much time to say anything,' I explained, still feeling the daggers emitting from Ron's eyes.

'You've changed the place quite dramatically,' Michael noted, looking around.

'Yes,' Gino agreed. 'We had the reopening party today, mainly for PR purposes.'

'What part of Greece?' Chef asked, returning to the previous conversation.

'Corfu.'

'Did you eat at Hannah's by any chance?'

'No, where is that?'

'Right in the heart of Corfu Town. The food is excellent.'

'Albert is the Chef here. He's our resident expert on restaurants,' I added.

'Hannah's? Doesn't sound Greek,' Michael replied.

'Believe me, it's exquisite. They specialise in regional dishes. The menu changes daily and every dish is prepared to perfection.'

As Gino, Chef and Michael discussed restaurants, Jane and I took the dishes into the kitchen.

'You didn't tell me that things had become serious,' Jane remarked, as soon as we were behind the closed door.

'They haven't.'

'You went to Greece with him and it isn't serious? Oh, come on.'

'No, really, it's just a…'

'Did you sleep with him?'

'Well, yes, but it's not commitment stuff.'

'Give it time. I reckon you two will be like Albert and me.'

'Then you two are still going strong?'

'Better than ever. His family was wonderful, made me feel right at home and Albert is just the best thing that's happened to me in a long while.'

'I'm pleased for you. I really am.'

'Thanks,' she said. 'I'm pleased too.'

On that note, Ron pushed open the swing door.

'Elizabeth, you really shouldn't have your friends visiting you at work,' she snarled, looking over the kitchen as if expecting to see something out of place.

'Oh, shut up Ron,' Jane snapped. 'It's after hours.'

Chef and Jane accompanied us back to Michael's house for coffee and ports. Chef and Michael had hit it off from the start, both being well travelled and avid collectors of artefacts. In particular, Chef was interested in Michael's African and South American pieces, saying he planned to visit Brazil early in the new year. Content to sit and talk, hours just passed without any of us realising the time. When Chef and Jane finally left, we dragged our weary bodies upstairs and crawled into bed, too tired to do anything but sleep.

Not surprisingly, given the amount of alcohol we'd consumed, we didn't wake until almost nine. So, rather than return to The Elms, I simply ironed the clothes I'd worn the day before. Thankfully Michael gave me a lift.

Arriving at The Gazebo, I noticed I was five minutes early.

However, on walking through the door, I found myself in Ron's line of fire.

'Elizabeth,' she screamed. 'Last night you and Jane left here without cleaning the toilets. Now I want you to get in there and tidy things up now. No excuses!'

I was about to mention the cleaner, but I didn't need to. Just as she'd finished speaking, a middle-aged woman came in the back door, armed with a bucket and mop, then disappeared into the ladies' restroom.

'That's the cleaner,' I explained, turning to enter the kitchen. Ron followed me in.

'What cleaner?' she asked. 'Since when do we have a woman come in to clean the toilets? We only have a cleaner once a week for the restaurant area alone, no kitchen duties and no toilet duties. Is that clear?'

'Listen Ron,' I answered, thoroughly tired of her power games. 'If you have a problem, you speak to Gino. He hired the cleaner, not me.' With that she abruptly turned and pushed through the swing door so hard it ricocheted back and forth, between the kitchen and the dining room, before slowing down and eventually closing.

As I sipped my coffee, I could hear Ron's raised voice emitting from Gino's office. I imagined he was feeling a little under the weather this morning and, by his aggravated response, her complaint had been ill-timed.

'I am the manager here, not you,' Gino retaliated. 'If I feel we need a cleaner, then I hire one. I don't have to obtain your permission.'

'But, it's a waste of money,' she tried to explain.

'The profitability of this establishment is my concern. Those girls earn every penny they receive and more. Besides, they are hired to handle food, not excrement.'

'I think you're letting them walk all over you,' she laughed, mockingly. 'What will they be expecting next, that you wait on the tables?'

'For the record Ron, I did wait on guests yesterday and not because Jane and Elizabeth weren't working hard. No Ron, it was because you had decided to play the role of a guest rather than an employed waitress. You are a member of the staff here and you are expected to serve patrons. If you abuse the seniority, you've been given again, you will be instantly demoted. Have I made myself understood?'

I couldn't hear Ron's reply because her voice was now subdued. After a few minutes silence, Jane walked into the kitchen.

'Did you hear Gino?' she asked. 'He certainly put Ron in her place. She just stormed out. Grabbed her bag and all.'

'Do you think she's left?' I asked.

'No, she'll be back. Just bluffing, I think.'

As Jane and I finished our coffee, Chef walked in with the week's supplies. Picking up the list we checked every purchase, before stacking the long-life products on the shelves and putting the perishables in the cold room. As a new kitchen hand had still not been hired, each day we were responsible for doing all the prep work, while Chef made the soup of the day and one pre-cooked main.

Today it was paella. We then tackled the tables, setting each one with linen, condiments and cutlery. By the time Ron returned, we were securing the daily menus inside the newly-designed folders, ready for the onslaught of lunch time customers.

The restaurant was booked to capacity today, mainly local businesses that had noticed the renovations and were keen to have a look inside. By their remarks, the general consensus was very favourable, with many customers complimenting Gino on the new look. Naturally he was delighted and, on counting the takings at closing, his wide smile revealed it had been a most profitable day.

Leaving The Gazebo, all I could think of was going straight to bed and not getting up for at least 12 hours.

2 September 1984

Even though food has been continually increased for the growing number of colony inhabitants, the subjects appear to fear their supply will diminish. That became very clear this week.

Over 100 subjects converged upon the second communal feeding area. They were also seen to be stealing food from some of the occupants. In all my years conducting studies I have never seen anything like it, where subjects have ready access to food and water yet somehow assume this will not always be the case.

In fact, going by recent developments, it would be reasonable to presume that these subjects are approaching hysteria with regards to worrying about food and its availability. Given that they are not at risk of any sustenance issues, this is a behavioural change of some significance.

Chapter 15

'About time you got home.' I heard the comment as I closed the door. Turning, I was astounded to see Fiona, sitting on her bed, filing her nails.

'You're back,' I said. 'Where have you been?'

'Nowhere in particular,' she shrugged. 'What about you?'

'I've been at work.'

'What all last night?'

'No, I stayed at Michael's. You, okay?' I asked, changing the subject.

'Why wouldn't I be? Honestly, I don't know who's worse, you or Angie,' she laughed.

'Yes, well, Angie was a bit concerned,' I explained.

For the next hour, Fiona and I chatted away. I filled her in on what had happened in her absence, but she remained tight-lipped about her own activities. After a while, we decided to switch off the light. We really had to get some sleep as tomorrow was already here.

For the remainder of the working week, everything went smoothly. Ron had calmed down considerably and had stopped questioning our every move. Gino was in fine form, revelling in the interest the renovations had stirred. Chef and Jane remained, as always, the perfect couple. Fiona was back but still secretive about Julian. Angie and Rick were devoted to one another. Brigit, by a stroke of luck, hadn't been seen for days, leading us to believe she'd secured another job. As for me, Michael was so caring and affectionate, I feared I was falling in love.

Come the weekend, I stayed at Michael's place. It was becoming a habit. Saturday was spent tending to domestic duties, our washing and grocery shopping. Saturday night we dined with Jane and Chef who we both now considered good friends. Sunday, we spent in bed, emerging mid-afternoon only to return a few hours later.

On Monday, Michael had a morning shoot so, with my bundle of laundry in hand, I headed back to The Elms. As it was already after nine, I was surprised to find Fiona still in the room. Her face was pale and she was hunched over the toilet. I asked if she was all right but she just waved me off, before retching into the porcelain bowl.

As I unloaded my washing, I waited for her to emerge. But she stayed in the bathroom. By the time she wandered out, her eyes watery, her face drawn, she looked like she should return to bed.

'Are you okay?' I asked.

'Yes, a bit of gastro, I think. I've had it for a few days.'

'Do you think you're well enough for work?'

'No, not really,' she said. 'But I have to go. They expect you to call first thing if you're going to be away.'

After dressing into her usual work attire, she said her good-byes. She looked washed-out, shaky and, watching her leave, I worried how she'd cope on her feet all day. Angie walked in some minutes later.

'How are you stranger?' she asked.

'I'm fine but Fiona doesn't look too well.'

'No, she's had some sort of bug. She hasn't gone to work?'

'Yes, she just left.'

'Well, that's crazy. She really ought to stay in bed until she gets it out of her system.'

'You seen Brigit?' I enquired.

'No, but I'm not complaining. It's much more comfortable around here. Still all good things come to an end, so don't be surprised if she turns up in a day or so.'

Our conversation was interrupted by Rick, waving a letter in his hand.

'It's been set. We go to court in six weeks,' he announced.

'Who said?' Angie asked.

'Madeleine. It says: 'Dear Mr Matters, the hearing for visitation rights regarding Edward Richard and Maxwell James has been set for Tuesday…'

'You don't need to read the letter, Rick,' Angie snapped. 'I just asked a simple question.'

'Don't tell me you're still upset about this. I thought we sorted it out.'

'No, you sorted it out Rick. I never got a word in.'

'So, what's the problem, then? Don't you want me to see my kids?'

'It's not that. I don't want you to get hurt and that's what this is all leading to.'

'Not necessarily.'

'You really are stupid sometimes,' Angie yelled. 'Of course, you're going to lose. You're going to be gutted.'

'Well thanks for your support,' Rick snapped, walking towards the door. 'I'll know who to call if I ever need a friend.'

With that he was gone, the door slammed behind him. Angie grabbed a cigarette, lit it and proceeded to look out of the window. I didn't comment, instead I busied myself with the ironing. After a few minutes, Angie spoke.

'Do you think I'm being unreasonable?'

'Maybe.'

'Why's that?'

'Well, expressing your reservations is one thing but you know, as much as I do, that Rick has to try to get visitation rights. If he doesn't, he'll never know what the outcome would have been. So, while you can share your fears, I think you should also respect his decision and be there if things don't go according to plan.'

'Hell, you're on his side.'

'There are no sides, Angie. You want what's best and he wants what's best too. So, seems to me you have the same objective.'

Wanting to clear the air, I wandered downstairs. After spending an hour or so in the lounge watching TV, I heard my name called and turning saw the manager.

'You're in the same room as Fiona?' I nodded. 'Well, someone's asking questions on the phone. Could you take the call?' Speaking into the receiver, I was greeted with a woman's voice.

'Hello, Sarah Evans here. I work with Fiona Rolland. I'm just calling to see how her father is?' I was momentarily taken aback.

'Well, Fiona hasn't told me the latest,' I said, carefully choosing my words.

'He hasn't passed away then?'

'Not that I know of but, as I said, I haven't caught up with the latest developments.'

'My father had a stroke many years ago. He didn't die but for a long time afterwards he was paralysed down one side of his body. I hope Fiona's father won't suffer like that.'

'No, of course not.'

'Well, Fiona left a message that she wouldn't be in today, but I was wondering if you had any idea when she'll be back at work. I know it's not the time to pester her, but I will have to arrange a replacement if she is planning to be away.'

'Ah yes, I understand. I should be talking to Fiona later on today, to ask her about her father. Perhaps I could get her to call you back.'

'Yes, I'd appreciate that.'

'Sarah Evans, you said?'

'Yes, thank you for your help.'

After scribbling down the name on a piece of paper, I wandered up to the room. As I unlocked the door, I was surprised to see Fiona on the bed glancing through a magazine.

'Has your father had a stroke?' I asked, walking over to her bed.

'Who told you that?'

'Sarah Evans, she wants you to call her back.'

'Oh fuck. It was just an excuse for not turning up. She's such a meddler.'

'No, I think she was genuinely concerned. She wanted to know if he'd passed away.'

'What did you say?'

'I said I hadn't heard the latest developments, so I didn't know.'

'Oh, good.'

'She needs you to let her know when you will be back, something about organising a replacement.'

'I'll be back tomorrow.'

'Well, call and let her know he's had a rapid recovery.'

'Or he's stable,' Fi suggested.

'Whatever, just make sure you call.'

'Yes, thanks. I will.'

The conversation ceased as Fiona went back to reading her magazine and I resumed my ironing.

'How are you feeling?' I asked, as Fiona opened a packet of crisps.

'Fine.'

'Still vomiting?'

'No.'

'Did you eat something that didn't agree with you?'

'Don't think so.'

‘Nothing tasted funny when you ate it?’

‘No.’

‘Well maybe it was one of those 24-hour bugs.’

‘Maybe.’

‘Did you have the runs?’

‘No.’

‘Pains in the stomach?’

‘No.’

‘Seen a doctor?’

‘No!’ Fiona snapped. ‘Honestly anyone would think you were a fucking doctor.’

‘All right, you don’t have to jump down my throat.’

The conversation stopped for a few minutes as I continued ironing.

‘If you must know, I don’t need to see a doctor. I’m pregnant.’

For a moment I was lost for words.

‘Are you sure?’ I finally asked.

‘Yes, I’m sure.’

‘Julian?’

‘Uh huh. And don’t you mention this to Angie.’

‘No, I won’t. What are you going to do?’

‘Well, I could always kill myself. Overdose on Angie’s pills over there.’

‘It’s not that bad.’

‘Isn’t it?’

‘You told Julian?’

‘Yes, I told him.’

‘What did he say?’

‘Oh well, he was wonderful about it,’ she answered, her eyes glistening. ‘He reached over and picked up his address book, then gave me the details of an abortion clinic. He had it written down under “A”. He’s done this before. Who knows how many times?’ she continued, a teardrop running down her cheek. ‘The worst part is I still love him. He’s an out-and-out cad and I still love him,’ she laughed self-mockingly. ‘I must be fucking crazy.’

‘What do you want to do?’

‘Oh, I don’t know. I’m 19. I live in this dump. I have no savings and if I told my parents, well my father would definitely have a stroke.’

‘Did you tell Julian when you went off for those few days?’

'Yes. But I wasn't with him. After he gave me the address, I was crying and he was worried I'd come back here and blab to someone. He doesn't want it to get out. He told me he couldn't possibly leave his wife. It would ruin his career. So, he booked me into a hotel for a few days until I'd settled down.'

'I'm sorry,' I said sympathetically, reaching over to pat her arm. Suddenly she burst into tears, sobbing into her hand.

'What am I going to do?'

'It'll work out,' I replied, stroking her hair.

'No, it won't. It's like a nightmare.'

'Well, that's because you've had a shock. But it will work out in the end, you'll see.'

In the midst of our conversation, Angie returned.

'What's the matter, Fi?' she asked.

'Oh, she's just been sick,' I replied. 'She shouldn't have eaten the crisps.'

'Gee, it must be bad,' Angie remarked. 'Hope it's not catchy.' With that Angie disappeared into the bathroom.

'Thanks, I'll be fine,' Fiona whispered, sitting up and wiping her face with a tissue.

'You're not on your own, Fi. I'll help you. Just tell me what you want to do and I'll help you.'

'Thanks, it'll be fine.'

The rest of the day was uneventful. Simone returned later and changed before going out again. There was no sign of Brigit. Angie chatted with Rick on the top bunk and Fiona kept to herself, the others assuming she was feeling too ill to converse.

When I awoke this morning, after a restless night's sleep, Fiona had left for work.

'Well at least that will take her mind off things,' I thought, as I prepared for the day ahead.

Arriving at The Gazebo, Gino asked if we could all sit down. He wanted to speak with us urgently. Gathering around a table, we listened intently as Gino addressed us all. Firstly, he spoke of the renovations, the recent upturn in business and then the profit projections for the next 12 months.

'As you can see,' he concluded, 'we are hoping to cover the cost of the refurbishment with increased business. With that in mind, I'm proposing we open seven days a week.'

By the look on everyone's faces, it was not a popular suggestion.

'What on the weekends?' Jane asked.

'Twelve hours a day, seven days a week?' Chef enquired, shaking his head.

'Wait on, wait on,' Gino continued, holding up his hand. 'Before you all jump to conclusions, let me explain. Naturally, I wouldn't expect anyone to want to work 12 hours a day, seven days a week. I wouldn't want to work that myself. In the past we haven't opened on weekends because it wasn't profitable to do so, the majority of our clientele coming from local companies and small businesses. However, now that The Gazebo has had a facelift, I believe we stand a good chance of picking up the casual diners. With the publicity our opening will spark, I'm confident Saturday and Sunday could be as profitable as the weekdays.'

'Yes, yes, we all accept that, but what is the bottom line?' Chef remarked.

'First of all, Jane, Ron and yourself work five days a week. I would like you to consider working Saturdays or Sundays, or even alternate weekends. Elizabeth you currently work four days a week. I would like you to extend that to five so that you're working every weekday, as well as consider the proposal I have put forward to the others. If you prefer not to work weekends, I will understand. I am quite comfortable employing additional staff for the weekend roster. However, I wanted to give you the choice. Are there any questions?'

'What rate of pay are you offering for weekend work?' Jane asked.

'Should you decide to work weekends we will negotiate a rate. Any more questions?' A pause. 'Good, then we can get on with lunch. It's going to be busy,' Gino added. 'We're already fully booked.'

Jane, Chef and I disappeared into the kitchen, while Ron hastily followed Gino, obviously wishing to ask a question.

'Oh great, there goes our social life,' Jane exclaimed.

'Well, it is optional,' Chef added. 'I will not be working weekends and I hope you won't.'

'Do we really have a choice?' Jane asked. 'Often what they say and what they mean are two entirely different things.'

'Personally, I think this is a little premature,' Chef remarked. 'Naturally business will sky rocket after a refurbishment but it generally is short term. In a month or two we'll not be bringing in the crowds we are today. The novelty will have worn off.'

For the remainder of the day, the conversation revolved around the proposed extended working hours. Ron didn't make any comment to us, but she had spoken at length to Gino in his office.

When Michael picked me up, I told him about Gino's suggestion.

'You're not going to work weekends? We'll never get to see each other.'

'No, I won't be working weekends. To be honest I don't want to work Mondays. It's only an extra 30 pounds, before tax, hardly worth the effort.'

'You get 30 pounds a day. Is that all?'

'Yes, two pounds 50p an hour to be precise, plus tips.'

'That's ridiculous. You're on your feet for 12 hours and you only earn 30 pounds?'

'Well, it's a job.'

'No, it's slave labour. That's what it is.' Once we were at Michael's house, we snacked on toasted sandwiches before going to bed. Lying in the darkness, the conversation reverted back to The Gazebo. 'You really have to leave there. Thirty pounds a day. That's not much more than unemployment benefits I'm guessing.'

'I can't get unemployment benefits. I'm an alien.'

'An alien?' Michael laughed.

'That's what they call immigrants here.'

'Do they?'

'Yes. I saw this sign outside the immigration building. It said aliens report here.'

'So, I sleep with an alien, eh?' Michael said.

'Well, you did say I was weird.'

'Oh, not back to that again. You've got a memory like an elephant.'

'Only teasing,' I added. 'Anyway, what makes people think that elephants have good memories?'

'Don't know. But how many times have you heard he's as happy as Larry. Who's Larry?'

'I know a Larry. But he's not very happy. He can be a little paranoid.'

'As paranoid as Larry,' Michael said. 'No, it doesn't have the same ring to it.'

Michael drove me to work so, thankfully, I was on time. Gino was occupied with phone calls and bookwork, keeping to himself for most of the day. Ron was subdued, lost in her own thoughts while Chef and Jane got on with the work at hand, neither of them commenting on Gino's proposal until just before closing.

'Have you spoken to Gino about the extended hours?' Jane asked, as we grabbed our bags.

'No, not yet.'

'What are you going to do?' she enquired.

'Well, I'm not working weekends,' I answered.

'No, we're not either.'

'What about your Mondays?'

'I don't think I have a choice as far as that's concerned.'

'You'd rather not work on Mondays?'

'Well, let's just say that financially it won't be that advantageous.'

'Yes, I know what you mean.'

When I arrived back at The Elms, Fiona was waiting for me. The others were all out, leaving us alone to talk.

'You offered to help me. You still want to?' she asked.

'Of course, I'll help. What can I do?'

'I've decided to have the termination. But I need someone to come with me?'

'I'll come with you. But you are sure that this is what you want?'

'What would you do?' she asked, nervously nibbling away at her fingernails.

'It doesn't matter what I'd do. You have to decide what you want. I can't advise you on that.'

'I know. I've thought about it. It's an awful decision. But I have to do it. It'll be better in the long run. Besides, what future could I give a baby? I'm a big baby myself.'

'Then I'll come with you,' I said. 'You just tell me when.'

'Thanks. I'll call them tomorrow. I'm going to the place that Julian suggested. It's in Surrey somewhere. I'll try and make it a Monday. You can't come any other day, can you?'

'You pick the best day for you and I'll work it out with Gino.'

'Okay, I'll see when they can fit me in, the sooner the better. You haven't told anyone, have you?'

'No.'

'Good, it's embarrassing. I'd hate Angie and Rick to know.'

‘They won’t.’ With that Fiona nodded, brushing her hair away from her face. She looked anxious and weary. ‘Try and get some sleep tonight,’ I suggested. ‘You look washed out.’

‘I will try but I keep tossing and turning and dreaming. I wake up every hour or so,’ she explained, biting her fingernails again. ‘Have you ever had an abortion?’

‘No.’

‘Would you?’

‘I don’t know.’

Come morning, Fiona still looked pale and drawn. I caught a glimpse of her leaving the room and, even from that distance, you could see the bags under her eyes.

Arriving at The Gazebo, my mind was otherwise occupied so I did what was required and nothing more. Early evening, Jane commented on my quiet mood.

‘Is everything all right with Michael?’ she asked, as we walked towards the kitchen, arms laden with dishes.

‘Yes, why?’

‘You seem upset. I thought you may have had words.’

‘No, I’m just tired, I think.’

Right on closing Michael called in to pick me up. When we were seated in the car, he commented that I looked anxious.

‘Yes, I’m worried about Fiona,’ I said. ‘Would you mind if I didn’t stay tonight? I want to see if she’s okay. She has a few troubles at the moment.’

‘Sure, that’s all right,’ he replied, a little cautiously. ‘You’re not upset with me?’

‘No, not at all,’ I answered, stroking his cheek. ‘I just have to talk to Fi.’

Unfortunately, Angie, Rick and Simone were all in the room. By the look on Fiona’s face, I knew she had made an appointment. As Angie chatted about her class today, Fiona kept looking my way.

‘Oh, I picked up that shampoo for you?’ Fiona suddenly said, indicating that I should go with her to the bathroom. Angie, Rick and Simone didn’t seem to notice that we were no longer participating in the conversation and continued on regardless. Once we were in the bathroom, Fiona shut the door. ‘This Monday at noon. We have to get two trains and then a bus. It takes almost two hours apparently.’

‘Do you have to stay over?’ I asked.

‘No, you’re just in and out. I should be allowed to leave by late afternoon. But they did say I’d need someone to take me home.’

‘Okay, Monday will be fine.’

The last day of the working week and I was exhausted. It seemed to take an eternity for the hangers-on to leave. It was well after midnight when I walked out of The Gazebo to see Michael sitting in his car.

‘Did you get another two pounds 50p for that extra hour’s work?’ Michael asked, as I slipped into the passenger seat.

I stayed at Michael’s all weekend. Just eating, sleeping, watching television and reading the Sunday papers. There was an article on the striking miners affecting market confidence. Turning the page, I noticed a feature story on The Gazebo, along with a photograph of Potter making his speech. The caption read: *Entrepreneur, Charles Potter, exposes his assets.* Apart from a brief mention of The Gazebo, the rest of the editorial was dedicated to Potter’s many and varied investments. The column concluded that Potter was still declining to comment on the Farrington take-over bid.

Towards the end of the day, Michael seemed a little put out that I was going back to The Elms. But I couldn’t worry about that. I needed to be with Fiona tonight. She had a big day ahead of her and I suspected she’d be nervous.

Chapter 16

Returning to The Elms, with my laundry, it was just as I'd expected. Fiona was agitated and pacing the room.

'Good, you're back,' she snapped. 'I thought you'd forgotten about tomorrow.'

'No, I haven't forgotten.'

'Well, we'll have to leave here first thing. You didn't tell him, did you?'

'Who?'

'Him!' she answered, throwing her arms in the air. 'That fella you've been seeing.'

'No, I haven't told anyone. I said I wouldn't.'

'Good!' she concluded, before abruptly disappearing into the bathroom.

Ordinarily, I would have been a little annoyed at Fiona's tone but, under the circumstances, I accepted her terseness without rebuke. She remained in the bathroom for an hour or so and I suspected she was probably crying. I could imagine how difficult the decision must have been and I was angry with Julian for deserting her at this time.

Come morning, Fiona was up and dressed before I'd even opened my eyes. Waking me, she said that she was going for a walk in the gardens, arranging to meet me in the foyer later. I showered and dressed then, with an hour up my sleeve, ventured downstairs.

'Elizabeth!' Tom called, as I entered the crowded dining room. In return I waved, grabbing my tea and toast before joining him at the table. 'Haven't seen you around,' he commented. 'I was beginning to think you'd moved out.'

'I wouldn't leave without saying good-bye. No, I've just been busy.'

'We've nearly finished the second model. Once you've done one, you get a feel for it. It's much faster the second time 'round.'

'So, the next one's your own creation from start to finish?' I enquired.

‘Yes, well that’s the plan. Jasper took my initial rough sketches and he’s been drawing up the design. Then from that he will carve out the sections. His talents really have been wasted working in a mine,’ Tom continued. ‘Larry’s right keen to get started as well. I’ve never known him to be so hyped up about anything.’

‘It can’t do him any harm,’ I added. ‘If he’s enjoying it, that’s good.’

‘You’re right there. It is good,’ he smiled.

For the remainder of the hour Tom discussed the idea for the model. Usually, I would have been interested in listening but this morning I was focused on Fiona.

Looking at my watch I made my excuses, before joining Fiona in the hallway. She was sitting on the bottom step, clutching a small overnight bag, obviously eager to get going.

The walk down to the tube station was tense, with Fiona swearing at the traffic and continually looking at her watch.

‘Will these damned lights ever change? Get out of the fucking way, you should be riding that bike on the road! Just walk in front of the cars, they’ll have to stop then! Move over, you’re hogging the pavement!’

It seemed that anyone who came within a metre of Fiona was in line for some verbal abuse. Strangers looked at her in disbelief as she bullied her way through the crowds, dragging me behind her.

I was relieved when, finally, we boarded the tube train, bound for the British Rail station. With so many commuters crammed inside, we were temporarily separated giving me the chance to calm my frazzled nerves. However, before I had begun to relax, it was time to get off.

‘The train to Croydon leaves from platform three,’ she stated, yanking my wrist so severely she nearly pulled my arm from its socket.

Storming through the crowded station, she stopped for no one, using her overnight bag to practically bulldoze anyone who happened to get in her way. Luckily, we only had to wait a minute or so, until the train arrived at the station and we were safely seated inside.

As the train departed the platform Fiona turned her attention to the passing sights, her persistent nail-biting hinting at the inner turmoil she was experiencing. Nothing was said as we journeyed towards Croydon, neither of us in the mood for small talk. Looking around, the compartment was practically empty, except for a few businessmen seated opposite and a woman with two small children. The youngest of the two children was standing, holding onto his mother's knee for support, while his elder sister gazed over at Fiona.

As the toddler's confidence increased, he took a few wobbly steps to the seat on the other side of the aisle. Turning to retrace his tracks he fell back, landing on his nappy-cushioned bottom. Looking over at the child, now endeavouring to crawl, his mother collected him in her arms before seating him securely on her lap. The other child, possibly around the age of three, still seemed fascinated by Fiona and eventually wandered over for a closer inspection.

Fiona smiled at the little girl then proceeded to look out the window, her sudden stillness indicating her obvious discomfort. Turning away, however, did nothing to discourage the child's attention and, for the next few minutes, she stayed focused on Fiona in a seemingly trance-like state.

'Eloise,' her mother called, noticing her daughter was staring. 'Come here, Eloise. Come here.' Even though her mother attempted to distract her, Eloise's eyes remained fixed. 'Eloise,' her mother repeated, but again to no avail.

'Your Mummy's calling you,' Fiona said, turning to speak to the curly haired child. 'Go and see your Mummy. Go on,' she waved. With that the little girl smiled then, touching Fiona's arm, slowly backed away. 'Kids usually hate me,' Fiona remarked. 'It's weird the way she was staring at me, like some kind of omen.'

'Are you having second thoughts?' I asked. 'It's okay, you know, if you want to change your mind.'

'No, I'm not having second thoughts. I don't win either way.'

Arriving in Croydon, I was surprised at the size of this bustling business area. Somehow, I had imagined it to be quite countrified. Opening a screwed-up piece of note paper, Fiona led the way to the bus stop. There we stood waiting for a ride to Wettherbene. Looking at Fiona, I noticed she was holding her overnight bag like a child would cuddle a teddy bear.

'What's in the bag?' I asked, suddenly realising I'd never seen her with this before.

'Clean underwear, sanitary pads, a change of clothes, that sort of thing, just in case something goes wrong and I need to stay over.'

'Oh,' I replied, turning my attention to the road and searching to see if the bus was approaching.

By the time our ride arrived we had been joined by four other women, all carrying these conspicuous overnight bags and each with a friend in tow. As we made our way up the steps, there were three more women inside with identical nervous expressions and similar luggage. Two matronly passengers shook their heads in disgust, as they watched the boarding group of nail-biting, bag-toting females.

'How big is this clinic?' I asked Fiona, counting the would-be patients before me.

'Don't know,' she answered. 'But we'll see soon enough.'

As the bus travelled along, the urban surrounds were gradually replaced by rolling hills and tree-lined roads, until the passing scenery was distinctly rural. One stop, two stop, three stops and each time a local would board, addressing the driver by name. After an hour or so, the bus swerved into a kerb, its tyres skidding on the stony ground.

Slamming the brakes hard, all passengers lunged forward then swung backwards as the bus screeched to a halt.

'Wettherbene Clinic,' the driver announced, and with that the girls lined up in single file, then proceeded to disembark. Looking at the bus, it was now practically empty leaving only a few of the locals to continue the journey on.

As the procession of young women walked down a small lane way bordered by hedges, we followed suit. On either side were fields with humble, thatched cottages in the distance. The lane way eventually turned off to the left, revealing an imposing, two-storey, brick residence ahead.

'Must have once been the manor house,' I guessed, looking at the size of the olde-worlde structure.

As the original property had obviously been subdivided, this large building was now allocated a meagre piece of land, providing a rather cramped car park for the clinic's staff and patients. Once inside, the ladies lined up at the front desk and details were taken.

'This is going to take all day,' Fiona whispered, who was becoming more uneasy by the minute. Eventually it was Fiona's turn so, to give her some privacy, I wandered over to look out the window. That done, we had to take a seat in a small room until Fiona's name was called by a counsellor. Apparently, it is mandatory that all patients speak with a resident psychologist to ensure they are of sound mind and have no doubts about their decision.

When Fiona was summoned, I leafed through the magazines expecting her to be some time. However, a little later she re-emerged, leading me onto the main waiting room. At first glance it looked like an airport lounge, what with the number of people seated and the collection of overnight bags. Even the anxious expressions could have been contributed to pre-flight jitters. I noticed that Fiona was carefully scrutinising every woman in the room and I imagined she was looking for similarities, something to make her feel more comfortable about the whole business.

As Fiona's name was called, she turned to me and nervously smiled.

'It'll be all over soon,' she said, and I nodded.

For the next hour or so, I gazed around the room. I discreetly ran my eye over the waiting patients, then the prints on the wall, the furnishings, the carpet, the light fittings, the panelled doors, even the cornices and ceiling roses. One hour became two and then three until I knew more about this room than the one back at The Elms.

As I was watching an ant roam along the skirting board, a nursing sister tapped me on the shoulder.

'Miss Rolland is ready to leave. She's waiting in the next room.'

Fiona looked pale and was still a little groggy after the anaesthetic. Grabbing her bag, I held onto her arm as we walked from the clinic to the bus stop at the end of the lane. Fiona sat down on a log while we waited for the rickety contraption to arrive. Unfortunately, it was nowhere in sight. Looking at my watch, I noticed half an hour had passed. But just as I was about to suggest hailing a ride from a local farmer, the tin shed on four wheels appeared in the distance.

Helping Fiona aboard, I purchased our tickets. By now, Fiona's face was a deathly, grey colour. Her breathing appeared to be irregular and beads of sweat were glistening on her forehead. Expecting Fiona to faint, I kept a constant watch over her as the bus slowly meandered towards the bustling town centre.

As soon as we had disembarked, Fiona vomited in the gutter.

Passers-by raised their eyebrows disapprovingly.

'Are you all right?' I asked, as Fiona wiped her mouth on a tissue.

'Yes, just feeling a little sick in the stomach. I need to sit down.'

Helping Fiona over to the bus shelter, I turned in search of a cab.

'To hell with the expense,' I thought, seeing Fiona was in no condition to travel back to London by train.

I hailed a few cabs but they passed without stopping. I tried again as the next wave of traffic came into view but my attempts were unsuccessful. Just as I was about to flag down another cab, a car screeched to a halt before me. Looking at the driver I saw it was Michael, as he switched off the ignition and jumped out.

'What are you doing here?' he asked, eyeing the overnight bag in my hand. 'You going somewhere?'

'No, it's Fiona, she's ill. Just had some tests done,' I hesitantly explained.

Michael glanced over at Fiona's feeble-looking frame, hunched in the corner of the shelter.

'Hop in,' he said. 'I'll drive you back to London.' Helping Fiona into the car, she rested her head against the cushioned seat. 'She looks terrible,' he remarked. 'Maybe we should take her to a hospital.'

'No, she'll be fine. She just needs to lie down. If you hadn't turned up, I don't know what we would've done.'

As we zig-zagged our way through the hectic peak hour traffic, I kept watch over Fiona. The colour was slowly returning to her cheeks but she still seemed very weak.

'Look, perhaps it would be better if she stays at my place. I don't think she'll get much rest in that room, what with everyone coming and going all the time.'

I glanced at Michael and smiled.

'Thanks,' I said. 'That would be better.'

On the approach to London, the traffic became congested. As the car crawled through one bottleneck after another, I wondered if we'd ever arrive at Michael's home. Fiona was now sleeping. Despite her open mouth looking dry and cracked, I was glad to see her getting some rest.

Outside Michael's place, I helped Fiona out of the car as he held the door open. Inside we walked her upstairs, removing her shoes and sliding her body under the covers. Still drowsy, she asked for a glass of water and Michael returned with one a few moments later.

'You don't want me to call a doctor?' I asked, as Michael left the room.

'No, I'm fine. I just need some sleep.' Walking to the door, Fiona spoke to me again. 'Elizabeth, I need a fresh pad. I don't want to stain the sheets.'

As I fetched one from the overnight bag, Fiona fumbled with her panties. Taking the blood-stained sanitary pad from her, I wrapped it in some toilet paper before dropping it in the rubbish bin outside.

Returning to check on Fiona, I saw that she was almost asleep.

'If you need anything just call.'

'Okay,' she mumbled, as I turned to leave the room.

I found Michael in the kitchen, busily preparing dinner.

'How is she?' he asked, rummaging in the cupboard.

'Oh, just tired, I think. She's sleeping.'

'You were the last person I expected to see in Croydon,' he remarked, filling a large saucepan with water.

'Yes? Well, you were the last person I expected to see. I had visions of myself trying to piggy-back Fiona to London.'

'I had a client meeting down there. It was only supposed to take an hour but it dragged on all afternoon,' he explained, popping the saucepan onto the stove. 'I thought we'd have pasta. Is that okay with you?'

'Yes, anything, I'm bushed.'

'So, what tests did she have?'

'Just gynaecological stuff, you know.'

'Oh, Wettherbene Clinic,' he guessed, and I was happy to leave it at that.

9 September 1984

Today I saw the doe named "Australia" eating something in her cage. On closer inspection she had the remains of what appeared to be a foetus hanging from her mouth. As there were no other pups nearby, I can only assume that she has eaten the entire litter.

This so far has been the most alarming development for a number of reasons. It is quite common for does in a colony to share the care of litters born to other mothers. That said, there is no evidence that a litter was born here. There is no nest in this doe cage. None of the does have been behaving as if they are pregnant. And because all bucks were neutered, they could not have inseminated any of the subjects.

While rattus norvegicus domestica does have, in very rare instances, mated with the rattus rattus species, the foetuses do not survive, with the dam miscarrying. This could possibly be what has happened here, in which case a doe in the cage would eat the pups for fear of their dead bodies attracting predators.

It is most probable that a doe is this cage has become pregnant to the wild rattus rattus that has been roaming the colony. But it cannot be ruled out that it is indeed another rattus rattus. Either way it appears, beyond doubt, that outside rats are still entering the colony or that subjects are escaping.

Yet, for all investigations, no flaw has been found in any of the cages or tunnels. At this point the only explanation is that foul play is to blame.

Chapter 17

After a restful night at Michael's house, Fiona insisted on going to work, even though I felt she should take another day off to fully recover. Returning with me to The Elms, we both changed into our work attire with Fiona hurrying off to catch the bus. As I was ready early, I decided to grab some breakfast before the dining room closed.

With no familiar faces in sight, I sat alone sipping my tea, thinking about the events of the previous day. I knew that Fiona would be fine physically but I was concerned she would suffer emotionally for some time to come.

Arriving at The Gazebo, I was summoned into Gino's office. He wanted my decision regarding the proposed extended hours. Feeling I had no choice, I agreed to working on Mondays but told him that weekend work was out of the question. As expected, Gino tried to talk me into alternate weekends, Saturdays or just Saturday nights. However, I remained firm and eventually he accepted that I could not be swayed.

'So, are you working weekends?' Jane asked, as I entered the kitchen.

'No, I told him it was out of the question.'

'Yes, so did I but somehow he's had me agree to alternate weekends.'

'What did Chef say?'

'Well, he's not going to be too happy when he hears. He's in with Gino now.' At that moment Chef walked in and poured himself a cup of coffee. 'How'd you go?' Jane asked.

'If you must know I'm fuming mad.' Jane gave me a sideways glance as Chef continued. 'He's gone and got me working every second weekend and I don't know how he did it.' With that Jane burst out laughing. 'It's not funny,' he remarked. 'It means we'll hardly have any time together.'

'No, it doesn't. We'll have lots of time together. I'm working alternate weekends too.'

'You too, how'd he do it?'

'Oh, I don't know. We're just not firm enough. Elizabeth stood her ground.'

'You did? I'm impressed,' Chef added. 'In future we better get you to negotiate on our behalf.'

The rest of the day passed without too many problems. Most of the time Ron kept out of our way, busying herself for the most part, flirting with male customers.

By closing, my legs were aching and I wasn't looking forward to the long trek through Kensington Gardens. However, Chef kindly asked if I'd like a lift home.

Arriving in the room, I found that Fiona had locked herself in the bathroom after having a blazing row with Angie of all people.

'God, what's got into her?' Angie fumed. 'She just about bit my head off.'

'Why?' I replied, looking over at the closed bathroom door.

'Oh, I don't know. I asked if she'd been with Julian last night and she flew into a rage. She said I was a big nosed, interfering bitch and to mind my own fucking business. Honestly, between her and Brigit, this place is becoming unbearable.'

'Is Brigit back?' I enquired, my eyes darting over to her bed for any tell-tale signs.

'No, but she'll be back. It must be this room. It brings out the worst in people.'

'No, it's just that she's not too well at the moment.'

'Brigit's ill?'

'Not Brigit, Fiona,' I answered. 'You know she's been off colour.'

'Yes, I know, but she's so hypersensitive. Honestly you don't dare to look at her sideways.'

'Just leave her alone. She'll come right again. You know what it's like when you're ill.'

Fiona stayed behind closed door for more than an hour. I didn't want to go to sleep until I'd made sure she was okay. I also wanted to wash my face and go to the toilet.

'See, she's even hogging the bathroom like Brigit,' Angie commented, after a while. 'I tell you it's this damned place.'

I ignored Angie, sensing that anything I said would only encourage the conversation and I really just wanted everything to return to normal.

Eventually Fiona emerged, nodded at me, and then hopped into her bunk. Feeling that my bladder was bursting I hurried to the bathroom, finding Fiona asleep when I returned.

Walking into The Gazebo this morning, Ron wanted to speak with us before we got down to work.

'What's it about?' Jane asked, as I dropped my bag in the office.

'I don't know but we'll find out soon enough.'

After we had both taken a seat at one of the tables, she held the floor discussing her so-called business proposal. Gino grinned as he looked over at the small gathering.

'Currently, we are all keeping our individual tips but this will no longer be the practice. From now on, all tips will be placed in a pool to be divided three ways at the end of the day.'

'You said this was a proposal. Sounds to me like you've already instigated it,' Jane remarked, her anger showing.

Not surprisingly the comment was ignored.

'I'll leave a bowl in the kitchen and please remember to place all tips in there,' Ron continued. 'If I find that anyone is keeping tips to themselves, I'll have their pay docked. Is that clear?'

Before either of us could refute this unreasonable new rule she was off, conveniently busying herself with a phone call.

Taking my arm Jane led me into the kitchen, deliberately slamming the door shut.

'Do you like this arrangement?' she asked.

'Don't be silly.'

'Then we don't go along with it. We'll place no tips in that bowl, neither of us.'

'What's going on?' Chef asked, busy stirring his soup du jour. As Jane explained, he shook his head in disbelief. 'If she did her share of waiting on tables, then she'd get tips as well. I don't see why you two should split your tips with someone who doesn't pull their weight. Speak to Gino. Sort it out now. It's simply a ridiculous situation, especially on the salaries they pay here. I'll be speaking with Gino myself soon. My assistant left months ago and they still haven't found a replacement. But do I get paid his salary? No, yet I'm expected to do his job.'

By the way Chef had sped up his stirring, the assistant issue was obviously contentious. Noticing the time, I realised that the lunch crowd would be converging on the restaurant shortly.

'We better talk to Gino after lunch. We have to set the tables,' I stated, nodding at the clock.

'Hell, where'd the morning go?' Jane said. 'Come on, we'll talk to him later when we sit down for our meal.'

'We haven't sat down for a meal since the renovations,' I said, following Jane from the kitchen.

'We will today,' she answered.

For the next three hours, Jane and I ran back and forth between the tables and the kitchen, as if we were competing in some sort of relay race. On the other hand, Ron led the customers to their tables and handed out the menus. The rest of her time was spent on personal calls. I noticed Gino staring at Ron as she giggled away on the phone, stopping only briefly to point out a table to an arriving guest. I could see he was not impressed.

As the last of the lunch crowd left, Jane and I went to collect our meals from the kitchen before sitting down with Chef for a well-earned rest. In Ron's absence, Gino had relished these friendly meal breaks and, after grabbing a plate of salad from the kitchen, he joined us at the table. Ron, still on the phone, curiously watched from a distance.

After the usual chit chat over a glass of wine, Jane brought up the subject of tips.

'Gino, if you expect us to share our tips, I think it's only fair that Elizabeth and I be given pay rises.'

Gino flinched. His discomfort with giving pay rises showing.

'I don't understand,' he said, looking at Jane with obvious bewilderment.

'If I have to give up a percentage of my tips to Ron and Elizabeth does too, we want our salaries increased. The pay here isn't good and we rely on tips to subsidise our living expenses.'

'But you don't share tips. It has always been the policy that the person who earns the tips, receives them. It gives everyone an extra incentive to provide good service. Hasn't that always been the case?' he asked.

'As of today, we've been told that we must share our tips with Ron. She's put a bowl in the kitchen and all tips are to go in there, then be divided three ways. Weren't you aware of that?'

‘No, of course not,’ he spluttered, glaring at Ron, who suddenly cut her phone conversation short. Ron, obviously realising that she was being watched, proceeded to tidy away the menus. But Gino called her over.

‘In a minute,’ she replied, pretending to be otherwise occupied.

‘No, now,’ exclaimed Gino, his face reddening.

As Ron deliberately took her time, Gino’s eyes darkened with the rage that was building inside him.

‘Yes,’ she said, sauntering over to the table.

‘I think this suggestion of yours regarding tips is worth consideration,’ Gino remarked, taking Jane, Chef and me by surprise. ‘But I must say that I prefer the policy we currently have in place. So, to make it as equitable as possible, I’ll work out an arrangement that will suit everyone. I’ll speak with you all about it at closing.’

Ron smiled, smelling the sweet scent of victory. Jane, Chef and I were utterly dumbfounded.

By six the dinner guests had started arriving, leaving us little time to discuss Gino’s strange turn around.

‘He’s lost the plot,’ Chef remarked. ‘If he’s not careful, he’ll lose three staff members as well.’

Jane and I agreed.

At closing I grabbed my bag then waited in the restaurant, gradually Jane and Chef joined me. However, Ron stood back until Gino was about to begin.

‘As I said before Ron, I am open to suggestions. However, I still believe that everyone who waits on tables should get the tips they have earned. That’s why I wouldn’t like the current policy to change.’ With that Ron frowned, while Jane and I breathed a sigh of relief. ‘So, to make it fair, because that is all you want Ron, I have divided the tables so that the three of you will be serving an equal number of guests. Ron you will be allocated all the small tables by the wall, giving you 14 customers to serve. Elizabeth you will take the three tables over there in the centre, as well as the tables by the kitchen, again a total of 14 customers to serve. Jane, you will have the larger tables at the back, that one by the office, as well as those by the entrance. These will give you 14 customers to serve. Are we agreed?’

‘Have you forgotten that I take customers to their tables, hand out the menus, answer the phone,’ Ron retaliated. ‘I couldn’t possibly handle serving 14 guests as well.’

'No, it's all under control, Ron. I've thought about that too. From now on I will take customers to their tables and hand out the menus. I will also answer the phone. It's not a demanding job. I can see the entrance from my office and I can easily pick up calls at my desk. So, you see, you have nothing to worry about. The three of you will now have your fair share of tips.'

Escaping Ron as quickly as possible, I left. Michael was waiting outside and, as we drove back to his place, I recounted the incident word for word.

'Fancy a coffee or a glass of wine?' Michael asked, closing the front door behind us.

'Coffee would be good.'

As Michael wandered into the kitchen, I dropped my bag on the sofa. Turning away a piece of lace caught my eye, stuffed behind the cushion. Pulling on the material I discovered it was a body suit; a black, silk teddy with lace inserts.

'You eaten?' I heard Michael ask, from the kitchen. As I held the lacy lingerie, Michael called out again. 'Want something to eat?' he shouted, his head peering around the corner. I turned and looked at him, somewhat bemused. 'Oh,' he said. 'Penny must have left that last night. We're doing a lingerie shoot. She brought over samples. Where'd you find it?'

'Behind the cushion.'

'Thanks, I'll give it to Penny tomorrow. She'll think she's lost it.'

Joining Michael in the kitchen, we toasted some bread and snacked until the early hours of the morning. If it hadn't been for the phone ringing, we would have certainly overslept.

'Hello,' Michael said, his voice unusually croaky. I could hear a woman on the other end of the phone. 'No, it's okay I had to get up.' I heard the woman's voice again. 'By the way, Elizabeth found some lingerie on the sofa.' Her voice said something indiscernible. 'Yes, that's what I said.' She spoke again. 'Okay, see you soon.' With that Michael hung up.

'Penny?'

'Yes, she said to say thanks. She thought she was going to be in trouble.'

Michael dropped me at work before heading off to meet Penny. The shoot would be ending quite late so we wouldn't be seeing each other tonight. Not that I minded, I really wanted to catch up with Fiona and make sure she was feeling better.

Arriving at The Gazebo, Ron was in fine form. Her expression cast in a permanent sneer and her tongue as sharp as ever. The lunch time crowd descended upon us and, as was the norm these days, the restaurant was filled to capacity. Ron attended to her tables slothfully, grimacing at requests, snapping at customers and generally causing chaos in the kitchen. Every second order she produced had to take priority because that customer needed to return to work urgently. As her orders were being filled, ours started piling up, until Chef took her to task.

'If I hear that another customer needs to get back to work within half an hour, I'll go out and ask them myself. From now on, Ron, orders are filled as they come in. No one jumps the queue.'

'If my customers want their meals quickly, they get their meals quickly. Understood?'

'Then you Ron will be cooking them. Understood?'

By the time I left The Gazebo, my head was throbbing. Ron's presence in the kitchen was unbearable. The air outside was refreshing, its coolness acting like a cold compress on my aching brow. Winter was fast approaching and the nights were now crisp.

'Should've brought a jacket,' I thought, folding my arms to warm my body as I strolled through Kensington Gardens.

Opening the door to the room, Angie and Fiona both raised their eyebrows at me, nodding to what represented my biggest dread. There was Brigit in a white night-dress asleep in her bed. Ducking into the bathroom, I washed my face and took a pain killer.

'The headache I had before was nothing,' I thought.

'When did she get back?' I asked, as I slipped out of my work clothes.

'This afternoon,' Angie remarked. 'Sorry you missed the welcome home party. She's apparently been at a conference.'

'What? The Terrorists' Convention.'

'Probably,' Fiona laughed. Fiona seemed calmer. Changing the subject to her day at work, I noticed Angie didn't ask too many questions, happy to just listen. Rick was asleep, curled up next to Angie. He was muttering something in his sleep. 'What's he saying?' Fiona asked.

'I don't know. He's saying blah blah blah blah Molly,' Angie answered.

'Molly?' Fiona enquired.

'Yes, that was the name of his dog. He often dreams about Molly.'

Next morning at The Gazebo, my headache reached a new pain threshold, as Gino announced the new hours would commence Monday week. Working so closely with Ron was suffocating. If anything, I would rather reduce my hours than find myself spending more time in her company.

As the day progressed it appeared that Ron was taking some sort of "go slow" industrial action. Spending an unnecessary amount of time to fulfil the most trivial request, she let customers wait up to 40 minutes for service. Eventually they were waving at any waitress in sight. I was about to step in and serve a few of her allocated patrons when Jane intervened.

'Don't you go serving her tables. That's what she wants.'

Following Jane's advice I kept to my own territory, politely telling the angry customers that they'd be served by their waitress soon.

As I left The Gazebo, expecting to find Michael outside, I saw Penny instead.

'Hi, Michael's been held up. He can't pick you up tonight. Fancy a drink?' In all honesty, I wasn't in the mood for socialising. However, as Brigit had now returned, I wasn't in the mood for The Elms either.

Penny drove us to one of her favourite haunts; a small bar near Piccadilly Circus. 'What'll it be?' she asked.

'Scotch.'

'With anything?'

'No, straight. Oh, get them to add some ice,' I said, changing my mind.

Penny returned with the drinks. Two for me and two for her.

'The bar here gets so busy. This'll save us queuing up later,' she explained.

'So, how's the shoot going?' I asked.

'Fine, Michael had to get the film off to the processors. The client wants to see proofs first thing tomorrow.'

'Oh, it makes for a long day, doesn't it?'

'Sure does, but what can you do? They pay the bills, right? So, how's it going with the two of you? Michael seems very contented.'

'Good, I think. We get along fine.'

'And Tanya's leaving him alone?'

'I don't know. He hasn't mentioned her. Why?'

'No, I'm glad. She really is bad news. A prized bitch if you ask me.'

After finishing our drinks, Penny dropped me off at The Elms.

'Thanks for coming to pick me up,' I said. 'You didn't have to. I could've walked.'

'My pleasure,' she smiled. 'See you soon.'

Everyone was asleep when eventually I stumbled into the room. The Scotch had been stronger than I'd expected. Waking up in the morning, I felt the effects of a minor hangover. Or perhaps, just the thought of seeing Ron was making my head heavy.

The last working day of the week and Ron still maintained her "go slow" tactic. Not that it really mattered. On Fridays, customers seemed content to spend hours over lunch. They usually didn't leave until late afternoon so, even though Ron's service was laggard, there were few complaints.

Michael had been delayed again and Penny once more, picked me up.

'This is becoming a habit,' I said. 'Listen, if Michael can't make it, it's no problem. I hate putting you out.'

'You're not putting me out. Honestly, I enjoy your company. Fancy a drink?'

This time we went to a club in Soho, where we drank until sunrise. By the time Penny pulled up outside The Elms, we were like best friends, laughing and giggling at anything and everything. Not surprisingly, I didn't stir until late afternoon. My mouth was dry and my hair stuck to my head, as if it had been greased back. Standing to go to the bathroom, I saw Angie sitting on her bed.

'I thought you'd be with Michael,' she said.

'No, I went out with Penny, his assistant. Boy she can drink.'

'So can you by the look of things.'

Returning freshly showered, I saw that Angie was about to take some pills.

'Didn't you just wake up?' I asked.

'Yes, but I have nothing else to do,' she replied. 'Rick has his nose stuck in these law books all the time. So, I may as well get my beauty sleep.'

'Did I tell you they've extended my hours at work?'

'No, why's that?'

'Business has picked up. They're booked out all the time. So, they've asked me to work Mondays.'

'Is that good?'

'No, not really. Next Monday is my last weekday off.'

'Well, come and meet me after class. I finish at midday. We could have some lunch.'

'Okay, I'll do that.'

Angie now had her eyes shut, drifting off to sleep so, leaving her in peace, I proceeded to dress.

Looking at my watch it was too late to hand in my laundry. Instead, I wandered downstairs. On the television, it was again bad news. All there seemed to be these days. This time about the number of companies going into liquidation. As I'd hoped, Tom was also in the lounge talking to Busman. They were both frowning.

'Well, you two look like you're discussing the problems of the world,' I said, trying to lighten the mood.

'No, we're just talking about Larry. He's gone all weird again.'

'Locked himself up?'

'No, worse than that,' Tom said, 'he's hidden the model. Won't let me go near it.'

'Why's that?' I asked.

'He said I was trying to steal it. Me? I bought the sodding thing. I tell you it's been a big mistake letting him get involved.'

'Well, you can't say I didn't warn you,' Busman said, 'and you should know by now what a moody bugger he is.'

'I was planning to have it finished by Monday but it won't be now. I tell you, it's the last time I let him help, the last time. He won't get a look in on the one I'm designing with Jasper.'

'He'll come to his senses. Just give him time,' I laughed. 'At least he's an interesting character, never a dull moment with Larry around.'

'I don't think it's funny Elizabeth,' Tom snapped, quite offended by my light-heartedness.

'No, I suppose not,' I answered. 'But it'll work out. You'll see.'

As Tom and Busman discussed model retrieval tactics, Rick passed the doorway.

'There's a message for you in the office,' he called, before turning to head off somewhere.

The message was from Michael. He was wondering if I was coming over. Stopping to call him on the payphone I said I'd be around about six then decided I'd better get ready. After a hectic week of shooting, Michael was naturally tired and suggested we eat in.

'I needn't have changed after all,' I thought but, in reality, I was pleased to be having a quiet night.

He showed me the proofs from the lingerie session and said there were more to come. By nightfall we were snuggled up together on the couch watching TV.

Over the last week, despite being summer, the weather had turned quite cool, hinting at the approaching autumn. Michael said this was nothing compared to winter but it felt chilly enough to me. Just as the climax of the movie was about to unfold, the phone rang.

'Hello,' Michael said. 'No. Yes. Yes. Ah, don't think so. Okay. I'll call you later,' and with that he hung up.

I was curious to ask who had called, but by the guarded way Michael had spoken on the phone, I guessed it was Tanya. The fact he didn't mention the caller to me, further seeded my suspicion. Perhaps Penny had been correct when she said that Tanya wouldn't stay away.

Suddenly the movie had lost its hold on my attention.

16 September 1984

There are so many incidents of hissing, huffing and biting it is becoming more challenging to keep track. Increases in these kinds of behaviour are up by over 400 per cent. Or, put another way, displays of aggression have more than quintupled. Furthermore, these incidents even involve bucks and does that, up until now, have been coexisting with few if any issues.

Neutered bucks have a significant reduction in testosterone which makes them less dominating. However, stress can increase a number of hormones that impact behaviour. Indeed corticosterone, oxytocin, vasopressin, dopamine and progesterone can be increased through tension and all have the potential to cause or trigger aggression. This could explain the surge in dominating behaviour among the does.

Further to increases in violent outbursts, the older of the bucks has been observed hoarding and has resorted to burying himself under the newspaper. In fact, his persistent digging, resulting in a build-up of paper, has now blocked his cage's entrance, preventing the other subjects from gaining access.

Chapter 18

Another lazy, stay indoors Sunday. Michael and I had reached the point where easy conversation was punctuated with comfortable silence, as hours came and went spent sleeping, eating or reading. At five, the phone rang. We'd experienced a cold front in recent days and Michael, in the process of lighting a fire, simply ignored the persistent noise.

'Aren't you going to answer it?' I asked.

'No, it's only the agency. They probably want me to call in first thing.' The phone rang a few more times then stopped, as Michael finally managed to get the kindling burning. After lounging about, listening to Michael's jazz tapes and drinking a fine bottle of red, we eventually dragged ourselves upstairs. Making my way to the bathroom, I heard the phone ring. When I emerged, Michael was sitting on the bed, with the receiver to his ear. 'Yes, that should be fine. Okay, I have to go. Yes okay. Bye.' I didn't need him to tell me who the caller was, his face said it all. 'Those agencies can be a right pain,' he casually remarked. 'They never leave you alone.'

First thing this morning I rushed back to The Elms. I was hoping to see Angie before she left for work, make sure that she still wanted me to meet her for lunch. Unfortunately, I'd just missed her and there I was alone with Brigit, sitting on her bed, putting on her shoes. I noticed Brigit's hand had been haphazardly bandaged. She tried to hide it from view before picking up her bag and hastily leaving the room. I quickly glanced around to see what could have caused Brigit's injury. But there was nothing broken and no sign of any blood.

'Why am I concerned about her?' I thought. 'I need to get ready and be out.'

I allowed myself just over an hour to get to Kilburn. However, it didn't take that long. As I approached the old church building, I noticed I was early and proceeded to wait at the gate.

Standing there, leaning against the timber picket fence, I saw a student leave the building with a bag strung over her shoulder and art pad in hand. A few minutes later another student came out. She was cramming something into her rucksack. Next came two more students and then another two. Despite looking up and down, there was still no sign of Angie but I could vaguely hear clapping and yelling from inside the hall.

'They must be giving a presentation in there,' I thought, imagining the tutor holding the floor. However, the clapping and cheering didn't subside. Instead, it seemed to be increasing in volume. Out of curiosity, I found myself inching closer.

Approaching the entrance, the racket filled the air. It sounded more like football spectators than a group of dedicated art students.

Arriving at the door, I peered around the corner, totally unprepared for the sight before me. As if re-enacting her Soho dance act, Angie was centre stage, twisting and turning her naked body in tune to the raucous response coming from her small but enthusiastic audience.

The students were laughing and nudging each other, yelling out for more as she happily obliged. With her back to the huddled students, she proceeded to contort in every direction, interspersed with a few high kicks.

As the gathering closed in, calling obscenities, Angie laughed and, then turning to the front row, rubbed her breasts into the face of a young man who was leaning forward for a closer view.

The show was now in full swing much to the delight of the juveniles. Next Angie squatted close to the floor and, holding her arms high in the air, repeatedly bounced on the spot to the beat of stomping feet. With unblinking eyes and panting mouths, the class looked on, more like peep show patrons than sensitive artistic types.

One of the students in the front row leapt into action and undid his flies. Not quick enough though, for no sooner had he unleashed his hard-on than semen ejected, spraying some of his classmates.

As more students started to undress, others were chanting "gang bang", clapping their hands in the air.

Jostling my way through the onlookers, I grabbed Angie by the arm. Then scooping up her clothes with my free hand, hastily pushed her towards the exit.

'What are you doing here?' she asked, as I slammed the storeroom door behind us.

'Lunch, remember. What are you doing here?'

'Oh, we're just having a laugh.' Then seeing my expression: 'God, don't be so serious.'

'Put these on,' I said, handing back her clothes.

Outside the jumble of voices and laughter eventually subsided until it was just the two of us in this uncomfortably confined space. As Angie began to dress, she broke the uneasy silence.

'Listen, it's the first time that's happened. Just got a little carried away. Audiences can do that to you.'

'So, where was the tutor, or did I miss him in the crowd?'

'No, he didn't turn up today.'

Lunch was a fairly quiet affair, both of us not really wanting to talk about the art class yet unable to think of anything else.

'You won't tell Rick?' she asked, as our meal arrived.

'No,' I said, but by my tone she could tell I was less than impressed.

'Look, I know you don't get it but I'm every bit an entertainer. Just not really cut out for this statue stuff.'

Arriving back at The Elms, Angie and I went our separate ways as Tom called me into the lounge.

'You seen Larry?'

'No, I've been out.'

'I think he's barricaded himself in the room again. I have to get that model.'

'Speak to the manager, Tom. He's the best one to ask.' After today, the model was the last thing on my mind.

Fiona was sitting on her bunk, obviously upset. Her eyes were red and puffy as if she'd been crying.

'What's wrong?' I asked. 'What are you doing home?'

'Julian came into the bar at lunch time. He just ignored me. Didn't even ask how I was. He knew I'd had it done and he didn't even want to know if I was okay.'

She blew her nose into a handkerchief.

'You can do better than him, Fi. Honestly. A really decent guy who'll be good to you and kind. One day, you'll wonder what you ever saw in Julian.'

'No, I won't.'

'You will. It's hard now but you will get over him,' I added, gently patting her on the shoulder.

Just then Angie emerged from the bathroom.

‘What’s the matter Fi?’

‘Oh, not well, that’s all.’

‘Gee, you want to see a doctor. You need something to clear it up. Can’t go on being ill all the time.’

The first day of the working week came around much too quickly. I struggled to rouse and eventually, forcing myself out of bed, stumbled into the bath and stood under the shower nozzle.

I turned on the spray, wet my hair, then grabbed hold of the shampoo, only vaguely aware of the heat emitting from its plastic outer. As I untwisted the lid something singed my finger, so much so I dropped the container and quickly held my hand under the running water before inspecting the damage. As suspected, my finger was blistering.

Looking down, I quickly jumped to one side and then out of the bath, just managing to save the soles of my feet from the scorching acid that was spreading, carried along by the water on its way to the drain.

Now safely standing on the bathroom floor, I filled the hand basin with water and submerged my seeping wound. Then it struck me what had happened.

Suddenly I swayed. My chest tightening. All air expelled from my lungs and seemingly no space left to replace it. I couldn’t breathe. My heart was racing. Completely panicked, I pounded on my chest to no avail. My mouth wanted to scream for help but no words came out. And then I gasped, clutching the porcelain ledge as I breathed again and tried to regain some composure.

I understood now why Brigit had a bandaged hand the other day. I couldn’t prove anything so there was no use complaining to management. Even the evidence had by now been washed away. I already knew she was not quite right but, as nothing had happened lately, I’d become complacent.

I managed to dispose of the now empty container with the help of Brigit’s towel. Then washed the fabric of any residue. I’m not sure why I just didn’t leave a little of her handiwork for the next time she wiped her face.

Feeling the others’ hair care products by the bath, I knew that Brigit had left theirs untouched. Needing a moment to steady my nerves, I sat naked on the cold bathroom floor. My body shaking not from the tiles but from shock.

Just moments before doing something, so seemingly harmless, like washing my hair could have robbed me of my sight for life. My teeth were now chattering. I had to get a grip, calm down or I would hyperventilate.

Suddenly I burst into tears, just as I needed to do, but careful not to let the others hear me. As this was a personal vendetta, I decided to keep it to myself. Brigit was no threat to Angie, Fiona or Simone so I felt they were better off oblivious. With the housing shortage where else could they go? As for me, I knew I had to leave. Next time, Michael mentioned moving in, I would accept. Until then, I would have to stay alert and keep all belongings locked in my case.

Arriving at The Gazebo, Gino mentioned to me that, as of next Monday, I'd be working five days a week.

'As if I needed reminding,' I thought, but nodded and smiled none the less.

Today patronage was noticeably down. For the first time in weeks, we weren't fully booked. Ron was furious because more couples turned up than groups which meant she was the busiest. However, Jane and I didn't mind in the slightest.

'I told Gino that business would drop once the novelty had worn off,' Chef remarked, in the kitchen, as he tidied away the supplies.

Personally, I felt that Ron's poor service had largely been responsible for the downturn. After all, who wants to wait 40 minutes to be served? Most businesses only allow an hour for lunch.

When it was time to leave, Jane invited me to her place for coffee. Chef was going to be there too. I told her that Michael was picking me up outside and she said he was more than welcome.

Michael seemed pleased with the invitation and proceeded to follow Chef's car to Jane's basement flat. It was one in a row of identical terraced buildings that line many Paddington streets.

Leading us down the stairs from the pavement, Jane unlocked the door and showed us in. The flat was warm, yet organised, a lot like Jane herself. With a sitting room that overlooked the stairs, a small hallway, cosy kitchen, two decent sized bedrooms and an ample bathroom, a sense of order prevailed, softened by some comfy cushions, table lamp and a rug by the hearth, all pre-loved enough to provide that homely feel. I complimented Jane on the decor but she told me that everything was already there, having rented the flat furnished.

We sat in the kitchen as Jane prepared the coffee, offering us some home-made cake.

Joining us at the table, Jane announced that Chef would be moving in next weekend and we both congratulated them on their decision.

'Yes, I've been living in Camden but it's time to move on. It's changed.'

'How so?' Michael asked.

'Hard to pinpoint. There's long been an undercurrent but I'm seeing more of these swastika-wearing, union jack-waving cocks; antisemitic, anti-black, anti-Asian, anti-gay, anti-authoritarian, anti-strikers, anti-Romani, probably even anti fat balding chef. Who knows? I was ready to get out. Besides, I'm spending most of my time here,' he continued, reaching for Jane's hand, 'so, I may as well be helping with the rent.' To my surprise, Chef and Jane had already arranged to get the next weekend off. 'We told Gino that I was moving in with Jane, didn't want him to hear it from anyone else.'

'Well, if you'd like help moving in, I'd be happy to lend a hand,' I offered.

'You can count on me too,' Michael added. 'With two cars it should make it easier.'

Next morning, as I arrived at The Gazebo, I could hear Ron's raised voice in Gino's office.

'It's unprofessional. You shouldn't allow it. One of them has to go.' Walking into the kitchen, Jane smiled.

'Did you hear Ron?' she asked.

'Yes, what's it about?'

'Albert and me, apparently Ron disapproves.'

'Who told her?'

'Gino did. I knew he would. He loves a good gossip.'

Our conversation was interrupted by Chef waltzing in with his supply of wine.

'She's demanding that one of us be sacked immediately,' he remarked, his eyes twinkling with amusement.

With that Ron barged into the kitchen.

'Have you forgotten there are tables to be set?' she asked, her question directed at Jane and me.

'What, do I still have a job?' Jane enquired cheekily, before casually exiting the room.

Lunch time bookings were down again. The restaurant was only half-filled and Gino looked concerned. He spoke to Chef about it when we sat down to eat.

'I've been thinking,' said Gino, 'maybe we should look at doing something with the menu.'

'We change the menu daily,' Chef said. 'What more can we do?'

‘Well, I don’t know. Perhaps we could have a theme for each day of the week,’ Gino suggested. ‘Or we could have an international month; one week Italian, then Indian, African and perhaps Japanese.’

Chef was shaking his head. ‘Won’t work,’ he stated.

‘How do you know it won’t work? It’s worth a try.’

‘Novel ideas like that just cheapen the tone of a place. We have always created menus using foods that are in season. That way the customers get the best produce available on any given day, and the restaurant doesn’t have to pay exorbitant costs. Personally, I think gimmick menus would be a mistake.’

‘Well, we have to increase business,’ Gino remarked. ‘I expected it to eventually level out but it’s taken a nosedive.’

‘Maybe it’s more to do with service than the menu,’ I commented.

‘What do you mean?’ Gino asked.

‘Perhaps we should be offering something the other restaurants aren’t. You could give regulars a VIP card which, I don’t know, gives them free coffee, a carafe of wine.’ Gino listened intently. ‘It seems to me that we should be encouraging our best customers to return.’

‘Yes, I agree,’ Gino said. ‘We could put together some kind of questionnaire, ask them what kinds of offers they’d like.’ As Gino left the table he called out to Ron: ‘Elizabeth’s had a marvellous idea.’

By Ron’s deadpan expression, she was not impressed.

Michael called to say he was going to be delayed at a shoot and that he couldn’t pick me up. But Chef drove me home. Fiona was sitting in the darkness, staring out the window, when I entered the room.

‘Don’t turn the light on,’ she said, ‘you’ll wake up Brigit.’

Looking over at Brigit, all I could see was the glowing whiteness emitting from her nightie. As my eyes adjusted to the dark, I could make out her folded arms and frowning face. Obviously, she was dreaming about me. Fiona kept her face turned away and I suspected she’d been crying again. Angie’s bed was empty and Simone was out. I needed to get some sleep but I couldn’t just leave Fiona to sit up by herself.

‘Did you see Julian again today?’ I asked. Fiona shook her head. ‘What’s upset you then?’

‘Her,’ she said, nodding her head towards Brigit. ‘Who else?’

‘What did she do?’

‘She complained about me putting sanitary pads in the bin in the bathroom.’

'I didn't know there was a bin in the bathroom.'

'There wasn't. I bought one.'

'And she complained about you using it?'

'She said they stink. She was going to dump them on the manager's desk,' she sniffed.

'Oh, you know she's a nutter,' I replied, handing Fiona a tissue. 'Don't worry about her.'

Fiona blew her nose so loudly Brigit roused slightly and turned over, only to roll onto her back again. Fiona looked tired and I encouraged her to get some sleep. After much convincing, she undressed and hopped into bed, removing her spectacles and blowing her nose once more before turning to face the wall.

20 September 1984

A doe was seen preparing to mate. Usually, a doe that is receptive will mate with a group of prospects, hundreds of times in just a few hours. The doe, in question, was surrounded by a gang of younger bucks. Prior to the experiment, they had undergone surgery to have their testes removed. But, as some of the young bucks were becoming responsive, I suspect there may have been outsiders in the mix. Thankfully though, another doe disturbed the huddle and they quickly dispersed.

Evidence of coupling has been observed in other cages as well. This is when a buck and doe try to separate from the colony in an effort to start their own pack. This is happening increasingly and must be in response to the soaring incidences of aggression. Perhaps these couples suspect that the only way to survive is to break free.

The biggest concern, however, is that sabotage is still taking place and I am yet to identify the culprit. The fear, of course, is that whoever is interfering with the experiment could start to release these newly formed couples, and a potentially significant development could be lost.

To this end I have endeavoured to keep access by my colleagues to an absolute minimum and never without supervision, even to the point of requesting they temporarily hand over their keys.

Chapter 19

This morning, Fiona and I awoke at the same time and decided to share the bathroom so we could breakfast together. I was looking forward to us sitting down to a chat without fear of someone overhearing. However, Tom insisted we joined his table.

While Tom and Busman fretted over Larry locking himself away with the half-finished model, Fiona fidgeted with her watch. When Tom started talking about calling a locksmith, Fiona bit her nails. As Busman suggested just knocking the door down, Fiona abruptly stood up.

'Is that all you've got to worry about? For fuck's sake,' she snapped, before strutting out of the room, leaving her breakfast half-eaten.

'Don't think much of your friend there, Elizabeth,' Tom commented.

'No, she's very rude,' Busman added.

I returned to the room to collect my things before wandering back downstairs. As I passed the office, the manager called me in.

'This arrived for you this morning,' he said, handing me a parcel.

It was small, light and wrapped in brown paper. My name scribbled in black ink. Sitting in the hallway, I proceeded to cautiously unwrap the item, worried that it might be something deadly, dispatched by Brigit. But there was no need to be alarmed. Instead, it was a crisp, white, cotton shirt from Penny. The attached note explained that she'd borrowed the shirt for a shoot. But because it had been slightly marked on the hem, the store wouldn't take it back. Hence it was a gift. She thought I could wear it at work. Naturally I was pleased. The shirt was beautifully made and obviously expensive. I made a mental note to get her phone number from Michael, so I could call to thank her personally.

Ron was waiting for me when I walked into the foyer at The Gazebo, her lips pursed and her expression pained like someone who had a shocking headache, or was about to inflict one on some unsuspecting passer-by.

‘I want to talk to you,’ she stated, turning to walk towards the ladies’ restroom and obviously expecting me to follow. There was no way I could avoid her all day, so I figured I may as well deal with whatever had upset her now. Entering the bathroom, I found her standing with her back to the basin. ‘Shut the door. This is between you and me.’ I obliged her request, though a little nervously.

‘What’s up?’ I asked, determined not to let her see my increasing anxiety.

‘Don’t you play stupid with me,’ she snarled, momentarily looking up at the ceiling before glaring at me with accusing eyes. ‘You’ve been after my job ever since you wangled your way in here.’

She stood, poised to pounce, waiting for a response. As she hadn’t asked a question, I was struggling with what to reply, but I had to say something. Otherwise we could be in here all day.

‘No, I’m not,’ I finally said. Not exactly a powerful rebuttal but truthful none the less.

‘You’re sleeping with him, aren’t you?’ she snapped, her face screwed up so tightly her eyes became lost in the folds of skin.

‘With who?’ I asked.

‘Gino. That’s it, isn’t it?’ I shook my head a little bewildered by the ridiculous notion, as she took a few steps towards me. ‘Well, you’re not the first you know and you won’t be the last. I’ve a good mind to tell his wife. She’s going to be working here. All I have to do is drop a few hints and you’ll be out on your ear. Your days are numbered, Elizabeth.’ With that she pushed past me and out the door, leaving me to ponder the entire bizarre conversation.

After dropping my bag in the office, I decided a coffee was in order, a good strong cup to soothe my nerves. Now that the initial shock had passed, I was becoming angry and I needed to take a few deep breaths to avoid doing something I may later regret.

Chef and Jane seemed oblivious to the conversation I’d just had with Ron and I wanted to keep it that way. There was nothing to be gained by dragging them in and making it bigger than it needed to be. I would much rather just put the whole incident behind me and get on with doing my job.

As the lunch crowd slowly started to wander in, Ron kept her eyes on my every movement. As Gino stopped to ask me about a customer I was serving, she scrutinised his expression. When he patted me on the arm, I saw her nod her head in acknowledgement.

By the time closing came around, I was happy to escape and half tempted never to return.

Michael was waiting out the front and I contemplated telling him. Ordinarily I shared everything that happened at work, however, this time I kept my mouth shut. I didn't want him to think there was any credence in Ron's accusations. The last thing I needed was for him to start questioning me as well.

Michael was very affectionate and chatty as we sat and ate a light supper, playfully twirling my hair, stroking my cheek and generally touching me at every opportunity. I asked him for Penny's phone number and he seemed a little taken aback, until I explained that she'd given me a shirt and I wanted to thank her. Spending far too long, unsuccessfully searching for the number, he eventually offered to thank her for me. I found this to be quite strange. After all, he must know Penny's number by heart.

This morning, after breakfast on the patio, Michael went upstairs to get his gear while I walked towards the door. I noticed the phone had been left off the hook and placed it back in its cradle.

'Tanya must be calling all the time,' I thought. 'How long is this going to last?'

Driving to The Gazebo, I was lost in thought. I figured that Michael didn't want me to speak with Penny, probably because Tanya had been turning up at shoots. Maybe he'd even been using her as one of the models. He didn't seem to want me to know that Tanya had been calling and, apart from finding this odd, it didn't overly concern me. Just as we pulled up outside the new exterior that was already showing wear and tear, Michael gave me a lingering kiss and told me he loved me.

Seizing the opportunity, I brought up us living together as he had earlier suggested. I needed to leave The Elms and this seemed as good a time as any to revisit his invitation. Now, though, it was Michael's turn to be taken aback and I could see he was searching for the right words to let me down gently.

Finally, he said: 'You know what? Things have been going so well between us, I reckon we should keep it that way. You're happy living with your friends and I'm working back so often, we wouldn't see each other any more than we do now. I'll see you tonight,' he said, before kissing me once again and giving me a hug.

I could have been bothered by Michael's turn around but, in truth, things were great, the best they'd been. If not for Brigit, I wouldn't have mentioned moving in.

The day wasn't as dramatic as I'd expected. Ron was away and even though we had to contend with the end of week crowd one waitress short, it was good to be occupied.

When it was time to leave, Chef gave me his address, asking if we could arrive around eight the next morning. I nodded and left to meet Michael outside. What with both of us having had a hectic day, we were thoroughly exhausted. Foregoing supper, we went straight to bed.

The alarm sounded at seven. We could have easily rolled over, and gone back to sleep, but we knew Chef and Jane were expecting us and we didn't want to let them down.

After quickly showering and dressing, we jumped into the car, narrowly avoiding the onslaught of Saturday morning shoppers. Using my *London A-Z*, I directed Michael down a series of decrepit-looking streets. Some of the shops we passed had been barricaded in iron sheets, and there was an abundance of litter being tossed about by the wind. Eventually Michael's car came to a halt outside number 73 and, looking around, we noticed Chef's car parked on the opposite side of the road.

On seeing us pull up, Jane emerged from the doorway and waved. Dressed in jeans and a sweater, she was sipping her coffee. Chef soon appeared behind her, still in his pyjamas.

'So, you had no trouble finding the place,' Chef acknowledged. 'I was expecting you to be late.'

Chef lived in a bed-sit on the ground floor of a double-storey residence. Venturing inside it seemed tiny, but that was probably because it was crammed with an assortment of objects. Chef was into collecting but, by the eclectic array of items, it wasn't clear what in particular interested him. It looked like anything and everything appealed to Chef.

Theatre posters, comics, Mexican pottery, fine bone china, a collection of stage costumes, a Samurai sword, a pianola, a stack of records, a hallstand covered in hats including a bowler, a Native American headdress and a raccoon-skin cap, an assortment of Asian idols, a collection of shells, fishing gear, an autographed photo of Winston Churchill, newspaper cuttings and framed tapestries filled every available space in the room, while an abundance of books lined shelves that covered the length of two walls.

'Does everything here have to be moved?' I asked, wondering how on earth we were going to transport the goods, let along fit them into Jane's flat.

'Well, I've told Albert he has to sort out this stuff,' Jane replied. 'We just won't have enough room for it all. That's what he's been doing this morning.'

The only sign that Chef had been doing any sorting was a small pile of items in the middle of the room containing an old woollen overcoat, a moth-eaten scarf, a pair of old shoes, a broken tea pot and a collection of metal pieces that looked as though they'd once belonged to a clock.

'I've been collecting this stuff for years,' Chef added, scratching his head. 'I can't just toss it out. Some of it's good.'

'Well, you can start on your clothes while I make Elizabeth and Michael some coffee. Would you believe he's got his football kit in there? He hasn't played since he was a school boy. That sweater can go for starters.'

'But it has sentimental value,' Chef explained.

'Sorry hon, we just haven't got the room. Now get on with it while I make the coffee.'

As Chef stood there looking around at the bric-a-brac, Michael grabbed a box.

'We could start on the books,' Michael suggested. 'There are a few car loads in this lot alone.'

By the time the coffee arrived, Michael and I had filled three boxes and we hadn't even left the top shelf. Chef was still dilly-dallying, his pile of discarded clothes so far only contained one more item; an outdated brown suit with wide lapels and flared legs.

'That can go,' Jane suggested, picking up a body shirt, 'and those,' pointing to a pair of red trousers, 'and definitely that,' pulling out a fake leopard skin jacket.

'They're coming back into fashion,' Chef exclaimed, keen to hang onto his treasures.

After hurrying down our coffee Michael and I filled another two boxes with books, before loading the car. Placing three boxes on the back seat and securing two in the boot, we set off with Jane's keys in hand.

'This is going to take all weekend,' Michael remarked, as his car accelerated up the street. 'I thought he'd already be packed.'

‘Well don’t expect too much progress to have been made by the time we return. He’ll probably still be contemplating the fate of that weird leotard thingy.’

The books were heavy. As Michael and I heaved the cumbersome load down the stairs at Jane’s place, we wondered what we’d gotten ourselves in for. Opening the door, Michael suggested lining the hallway with the boxes. So, taking the bursting cardboard cartons to the rear of the flat we proceeded to stack them. That done, we locked up and headed back to Camden.

On our return, Chef was still in his pyjamas, slowly sorting through the wardrobe stuffed full with outdated clothing. Jane had proceeded to pack away the china, carefully wrapping each piece in newspaper before placing it inside a box. For the next half an hour, Michael stood on a chair and handed down one book after another as I rapidly filled another five boxes. That done we each had a glass of water before hitting the road again.

The hallway at Jane’s was a quarter filled by the time we had stored our latest load.

‘I don’t know how they’re going to fit everything in,’ Michael said. ‘Perhaps we should clear aside the bed in that spare room and just place everything in there. They won’t be able to move otherwise.’

‘Oh, they’ll sort it out, let’s just keep going,’ I answered frustratingly.

Back in Camden and the only notable sign of progress was that Chef had dressed. Jane was still packing the same box with china, leaving Chef to ponder the future of a patchwork, knitted vest that belonged to the days of flower power, peace and brotherly love.

Without delay, Michael and I busily worked on the next shelf filling another six boxes with the heavy, dusty works of Dickens, D.H. Lawrence and Shakespeare, as well as some lesser-known authors. Into the car these went, along with the Native American headdress, a pile of Phantom comics and a roll of theatre posters, thrown in at the last moment to fill up the remaining floor space. Like a well-oiled machine, we unpacked the car. By now we had mastered the art of walking down the steps without losing our footing. We stopped to grab a glass of water before returning to Camden.

For the next five hours, Michael and I drove back and forth, only stopping to fill the tank with petrol. In that time Jane had barely managed to pack four boxes, while Chef had only sorted through his wardrobe, tossing out a total of eight pieces of clothing.

‘Hardly worth the time or energy,’ I thought.

Looking around at the empty book shelves, I could at least see some results for our efforts. Not that we needed proof. Our bruised, sore and weary bodies were letting us know, in no uncertain terms, that we had pushed ourselves to the limit.

As Chef and Jane loaded their car, Michael and I proceeded to fill another six boxes, making sure to include enough padding to protect the fragile items. Over the boxes, Michael laid as many of Chef's clothes as the car could handle, without restricting his vision through the rear-view mirror. With both cars filled to capacity, we set off once again across town.

Jane seemed astounded by the number of boxes already stacked in her flat.

'We can't possibly bring everything over,' she remarked, shaking her head. 'There's not going to be enough room.'

Michael suggested moving the bed in the spare room, upright against the wall, and placing everything in there. After an unnecessary amount of discussion, the four of us did just that.

The trip back to Camden was becoming monotonous. Even Michael could have driven there with his eyes closed by now. Again, we packed more boxes, becoming less pedantic as time went on. Then, in two overburdened vehicles, we set off with seemingly no end in sight to this tedious ordeal.

'They're like a pair of snails,' Michael exclaimed, obviously annoyed, before honking the horn at a car that had swerved into our path.

It was now dark and Saturday night revellers were heading out to the restaurants, theatres and bars. The only place I wanted to head for was bed and, by the look of things, I wouldn't be doing that any time soon.

Come nine we were still repeating the tiresome trek. My hands were filthy from a combination of dust and newspaper print. I was also famished. Thankfully, Chef informed us that the furniture was to remain in Camden. By my estimations, there were only another two trips to go before we could call it a night.

It was late when we finally heaved in the last of the boxes, filling the remaining available floor space in Jane's flat. Chef returned to his car, telling us he'd stopped on the way to buy supper. This was his favourite dish apparently so naturally we were curious, expecting some type of elaborately prepared treat, and wondering where he managed to get such a meal at this time of night. It turned out to be fish and chips that we ate from the wrapper, along with cans of fizzy drink and chocolate bars for sweets.

It was almost dawn when Michael and I eventually crawled under the covers, and the sun was setting when we prized our heavy eyelids open. After showering and snacking on leftover pasta we went back to bed, not stirring again until the alarm sounded.

As expected, every muscle was aching. Michael felt much the same way, so it took an eternity to ease our fragile bodies into the car seats. Michael groaned as he placed the car into first gear, his legs obviously worse for wear after climbing so many stairs. As soon as I laughed, I wished I hadn't, my abdominals painfully complaining.

'This is the last time I help anyone move. The last time,' Michael exclaimed.

I quietly agreed.

Chapter 20

Monday at The Gazebo was a quiet affair. With so few customers to serve, I wondered why I'd been asked to work the extra day. Not surprisingly, Chef and Jane showed no signs of muscle strain or fatigue. They even had the nerve to comment how easy the move had been.

Michael was working late again so come closing I headed off, folding my arms tightly to shield myself from the biting wind and damp night air.

Walking through Kensington Gardens I wondered how I'd manage this long trek in the midst of winter, with snow piled around my ankles and icy pavements. Must invest in a thermal jacket, I decided, my teeth chattering with the gripping cold that froze my bones and numbed my flesh.

The Elms provided an inviting sight as I dragged my feet the final, torturous stretch. Escaping the howling wind, I took cover in the hallway, my ears ringing from exposure to the elements. Just then I noticed something glistening on the floor. I reached down and picked it up, expecting it to be some kind of jewellery. It wasn't. Instead, I was holding a miniature, brass ship's wheel. Tom must have dropped it moving the model. I looked at my watch. He should still be up. So, I climbed the stairs to his floor. There was music coming from his room. I knocked on the door and it opened. Pushing on it, I looked in.

The room was in darkness and the bunk beds were empty. The only light was a thin slither emitting from the bathroom. Stepping inside I called his name. No reply. But the music was quite loud. The bathroom door was ajar and I could see the mirror. I stepped closer, craning my neck, to see if Tom was inside. From the reflection I could see he was and Jasper. They were standing naked by the running shower, kissing ever so gently. I moved so as not to be seen. Then very slowly and, as quietly as I could, back tracked to the door, making sure that when I left it was shut tight behind me. We all have so little privacy; I didn't want to disturb. I would return the ship's wheel tomorrow.

'Hell, it's cold out there,' I said, speaking to Fiona. She was the only one in the room when I unlocked the door.

'You haven't seen anything yet,' Fiona remarked, sitting on the bed peeling a banana. 'Wait until winter strikes. Then you'll know what cold is.'

'Where's everyone?' I asked.

'Don't know. Brigit's at work. But as for Angie and Simone, they could be anywhere.'

'Oh,' I said, 'hope they're rugged up.'

Fiona seemed distracted, lost in her thoughts. She kept eyeing me as if she wanted to speak. But then she'd change her mind, taking a bite of the banana instead. 'Is something up?' I asked, as I undressed. 'Did you see Julian?'

'No,' she shook her head. 'No, nothing's up.' Disappearing into the bathroom to brush my teeth, I noticed Fiona's shape hovering in the doorway. As I wiped my mouth, she went to speak but then walked back into the room. After washing my face and tying my hair in a scrunchy, I switched off the bathroom light before jumping into bed. 'Were you with Michael all weekend?' Fiona curiously asked. 'The whole time?' she added.

'Yes, since last Thursday. Why? Were you looking for me?' I said, fumbling under the duvet to remove my socks.

She shook her head, took a bite of her banana and then spoke again when her mouth was empty.

'So, everything's going well? No problems?'

'No, no problems. He's fairly easy going, well you've met him,' I replied, plumping my pillows to make them comfortable.

'So, you're still together?' Fiona asked, as I settled in and straightened the bedding.

'Sure,' I answered, wondering why she was suddenly interested. I glanced over at Fiona who, having finished her banana, was now playing with the leftover peel, flicking it back and forth repeatedly. 'What's up Fi? You seem all edgy.'

'Well, I don't want to tell you something yet if I don't tell you I wouldn't be much of a friend and I am a friend so I must tell you.' I was staggered by Fiona's blurted reply, especially as she had delivered the entire monologue without stopping to take a breath. 'Michael's seeing someone.' I stared at her dumbfounded. 'He is,' she continued. 'I saw them in the bistro at work. I didn't want to tell you but I didn't want not to tell you. You're not angry with me, are you?'

'Fi, Michael often takes women out to lunch. It's probably a client. Really, he's even brought a client to The Gazebo.'

'This wasn't a client. They were...They were...They were all over each other. Touching under the table, you know what I mean.'

'Was she blonde?'

'Uh huh. She had blonde hair in a bun, small features. They obviously knew each other well.'

'When was this?'

'Thursday lunch. He didn't see me but I knew it was him. I recognised him straight away. I wouldn't have even seen him, only I walked into the bistro to get some clean glasses.' I listened without answering, a little taken aback. 'Are you okay?' she asked.

'Yes.'

'You're not mad at me?'

'No.'

'I'm sorry,' she said. 'Sure you're okay?'

'Yes, I'm fine. Thanks for telling me.'

Fiona went to sleep a short time afterwards but I stayed awake for some hours. It was Tanya, I knew that. But I couldn't understand the sudden turn around. Lately Michael had been so affectionate, touching me at every opportunity, telling me that he loved me.

'Must be the guilts,' I thought.

Come morning I was surprisingly optimistic. As I showered, I thought about everything Fiona had said. In reality, Fiona probably wouldn't recognise Michael. She had only seen him once and she was recovering from an anaesthetic at the time. Besides, the bar where Fiona worked was frequented by business people. Hardly the type of place you'd go on a date. After careful consideration, I assumed that Fiona had been mistaken. It wasn't Michael she'd seen at all, just someone who looked like him.

Again, work was much quieter than expected. After lunch, Gino showed me the list of questions he intended to ask customers. I perused his strange handwriting, asking him to clarify the odd word here and there. When I admitted it sounded good, he smiled. Turning away I saw that Ron had been watching us from the corner.

Early evening, in the midst of dinner, Gino handed me a message. Michael would be working until the early hours and couldn't pick me up as previously arranged. I thanked Gino and continued serving guests.

Later that night, as I left The Gazebo, Chef and Jane watched me walk up Queensway.

'Do you want a lift?' Jane called.

'No, thanks,' I replied, yelling to be heard over the traffic. 'The walk will do me good.'

Arriving in the room, I found Angie pacing back and forth, waving a piece of paper.

'I feel like phoning the old codger myself. Tell him he doesn't have to sack me because I don't want his fucking job, not with his upstart students and all their high and mighty ways. That's what I'll do, I'll ring the cock. Like hell, he can tell me my services aren't wanted any more. He hasn't seen…'

Suddenly Angie stopped when she noticed me standing there.

'You lost your job?' I asked.

'Yes, so what? It was worse than standing in a sodding store window. You're nothing more than a mannequin.'

'Why? Did he find out about the other day?' I asked, dropping my bag on the bed.

'No, don't think so,' she answered, throwing her hands in the air. 'Just not their sort I suppose. Not a Sloane Ranger. Not a rich daddy's girl. Who knows why?'

'They didn't tell you? If they've dismissed you, the very least you'd expect is a reason.'

'Yes, Elizabeth's right,' Fiona agreed, 'they really should have told you why.'

'It doesn't matter. Don't want to know. Truth is I was going to leave anyway. It's never been for me. You'd have to be brainless to want to earn a living by standing still.'

With phone message in hand, Angie went to the bathroom, shutting the door behind her.

'She's upset,' Fiona acknowledged. 'She liked working, told me so.'

'I know,' I said, sitting down to remove my shoes.

'Heard from Michael?'

'Yes, he called to say he'd be working late.'

'Working late,' Fiona repeated. 'Hope you told him to go to hell.'

'I didn't speak to him. I was working. Gino took a message.'

'So, when are you going to tell him?'

'What?'

'To go to hell.'

'Oh, I don't know.'

'If you go over there now, you'll catch him in bed with her.'

'I'm hardly going to walk over now. It's past midnight.'

'That's what I mean, they'll be in bed.'

'No there's a time and a place. It can wait.' The conversation died as I proceeded to undress.

'Saw Julian again,' Fiona whispered.

'He came in?'

'Yes.'

'Did he speak to you?'

'Are you joking? I've become the invisible woman.'

'How do you feel?'

'Awful. It hurts every time I see him. I don't think I can continue working there.'

'You're going to look for another job?' I asked, The Gazebo coming to mind.

'No, I think I'd rather go home. Just for a while. Find my feet again.'

'What, soon?' I asked, saddened by the prospect of losing a friend.

'Yes, I think so. There's nothing here for me really. I think I need to get away from the Julians and the Brigits of this world, even those two fellas downstairs, your friends. It's all so depressing around here.'

Angie emerged from the bathroom, cutting our conversation short.

'Listen I'm going to tell Rick that I packed it in. They weren't paying me on time. They owed me money or something. So, keep it to yourselves okay. God, it's made me seething mad. But I can rise above it eh? I'm better than this, I am.'

As Angie hopped up to the bunk, she lit a cigarette and looked out the window.

'Where's Rick?' Fiona asked.

'He's playing law, what else?'

'When's the hearing?' Fiona continued. 'It must be soon.'

'Next Tuesday,' Angie mumbled, her yawn indicating disinterest.

'You can go with him,' I said, 'now you're not working.'

'Yes, I suppose, haven't decided. Anyway, it's not really up to me. It has to be what Rick wants. It's only what Rick wants that counts.'

'That's a bit rough,' Fiona replied.

'Listen, who's sticking their interfering big nose in now? You told me to mind my own business, so how about you minding yours?'

After that the conversation ended. Everyone seemed to be on tenterhooks these days; Ron, Tom, Larry, Fiona and Angie. It was times like this I craved the privacy of my own room.

The rest of the working week continued without major incident.

Friday morning, before I left for work, Simone told me she'd heard that we were getting another roommate. They were replacing Brigit's single bed with a bunk that day. It was just as Tom had predicted and already most rooms had gained an extra tenant. We were among the last.

I didn't manage to escape from The Gazebo until almost midnight. Michael was waiting outside. I hadn't seen him since Monday morning, his work schedule having been unusually hectic. Michael smiled as I opened the car door, then leant across to kiss me. Naturally, I wasn't overly responsive and pulled my face away much sooner than he expected.

'You, okay?' he asked. 'Tired?'

'Yes, I'm dead, can't wait to get some sleep.'

Surprisingly, Michael's demanding week had done little to diminish his libido. Yet no amount of coaxing or fondling, kissing or caressing could entice me to do anything other than sleep.

Saturday morning, I told Michael I was coming down with something and returned to The Elms.

Walking into the room, I noticed someone was sitting on the bunk addition above Brigit's spot. Obviously, our new roommate. Tall with a wiry frame, her head was flanked by tight, black curls while her teeth glowed white against her dark skin. Introducing herself as Hettie, she told me she was from Guyana and would be staying for a week. I, in turn, introduced myself and told her I'd be staying forever. At that admission she smiled, unsure if I was joking or not.

Hettie entertained me for the next hour or so with travelling anecdotes. She had spent the past three months hitchhiking through Europe and this was the final stop before returning home. A nurse, she worked in the local hospital and was interested in trying her hand at midwifery. With that objective in mind, she'd enrolled for extra study in the new year. In the midst of our tete-a-tete, Brigit walked in, nodded at the new roommate before disappearing into the bathroom.

'Who's that?' Hettie asked.

'Brigit, she sleeps beneath you.'

Just then, Fiona pushed open the door.

'Fucking hell, she knew I was behind her,' Fiona complained, struggling to enter the room, her arms laden with groceries. 'She could've held it open for me.'

'This is Hettie, our new roommate,' I explained.

'Hi,' Fiona said, dropping her shopping bags onto the bunk. 'Did you tell him last night?' she asked, turning to me.

'No.'

'Why?'

'It wasn't the right time.'

'You didn't do anything with him?' Fiona enquired, not wanting to say too much in front of Hettie.

'No, I told him I was feeling off colour.'

'Good,' Fiona nodded approvingly.

After dropping off my washing at the nearby laundromat, Hettie, Fiona and I sat down in the local cafe and enjoyed a light lunch. It was refreshing to have a new face in the room, especially one with so many experiences to share. Returning, Timothy seemed less than impressed with the new resident, refusing to move his feet as we approached. As she stepped over his outstretched legs, he said something to Hettie.

'What did he say?' I asked, as we climbed the stairs.

Hettie just shrugged.

The rest of the day was spent in the room. Strangely I was feeling a little under par. Perhaps I was being punished for lying to Michael.

Come night time, Fiona and I were alone in the room. After reading for a while, we switched off the light and tried to get some sleep.

'I resigned on Friday,' Fiona admitted, in the darkness.

'Yesterday, shouldn't you give it some time, think about it for a while?'

'No, I've spoken to Mum. She knows I'm coming home; reckons they're looking for people at the local pub.'

'Oh, Fi,' I said, disappointed by the news.

'Now don't you go getting all soppy. It's for the best. Who knows I might come back? Just need a break that's all.'

'You won't come back, will you?'

The room was silent as I waited for a reply.

'No, probably not.'

Sunday, I was well under the weather with a fever and a headache to boot. Fiona gave me some pain killers, Simone offered to go to the shop to buy soup, Angie said she'd share her sedatives and Hettie recommended rest.

As Rick was lost in law books Angie went out with Peter, Rick's roommate. They were planning to visit Peter's elderly parents for the day.

Fiona had taken to walking. She said it cleared her head. After donning a pair of running shoes, she headed off for a brisk walk to Covent Garden and back. Considering the distance involved, I doubted it would be brisk, imagining Fiona dragging her body back on all fours, if indeed she returned at all.

With just one week in London, Hettie was keen to see the sights and left around the same time as the others.

Brigit wasn't in the room either, probably at work.

With everyone out, I took two pain killers and two of Angie's sedatives before pulling up the covers and drifting off.

As I slept, I was vaguely aware of a scratching noise. A scraping sound that would start and then stop, before beginning once more. It seemed to be close by. Though, in my hazy state, the distance was unclear. Each time I roused, I'd attempt to open my eyes, determine the source of the sound. But my eyes remained sealed and I drifted off again.

Sometime later I was aware of banging, shouting and swearing.

Suddenly someone had my shoulders, shaking my body angrily. Eventually forcing my eyelids apart, I saw the blurred image of Fiona standing over my bed. With sweat trickling down her face, she was ranting and raving, pointing to something as she spoke. Rubbing my eyes, I pulled myself up into a sitting position. But, as hard as I tried, I couldn't see any reason for her overbearing behaviour.

Grabbing me by the arm, she virtually pulled me out of bed and led me to the door. My feet stumbled over the discarded bedding as I endeavoured to gain my balance. Fiona was now pointing to the door, as I adjusted my eyes to the light streaming in from the hallway.

Looking I could make out something, but I wasn't sure what it was. Someone had scraped paint off the cream-coloured door, revealing the patchy undercoat in places.

'Can you believe this place?' Fiona was yelling, angrier than I ever remember seeing her before. I realised that someone had vandalised the door but, considering the state of The Elms, I felt she was over-reacting. 'I'm going to report them, call the police. People like this have to be jailed. What's the matter with everyone?'

I turned away from the doorway, the light in the hallway temporarily blurring my vision. After rubbing my eyes, I focused on the door once more and saw what had riled Fiona. There in front of me was a swastika, roughly carved into the panelled door. The floor littered with the rejected dried paint.

'Who did that?' I asked.

'You don't know? Didn't you hear anything?' she asked.

'Yes, I heard scraping but I was half asleep, Angie's pills are paralysing. Honestly, I don't know how she takes a handful.'

With that Fiona turned on her heel and walked towards the stairway.

'I'm speaking with the manager,' she yelled, 'fascist pig.' Walking back to my bunk, I collected the bed covers from the floor before sitting down. I was still woozy from Angie's so-called harmless sedatives and vowed never to take them again. Fiona arrived back with the manager in tow. 'This is what that weirdo's done,' she said, pointing to the evidence. 'I want him evicted.'

The manager looked at the damaged door, running his finger along the roughly etched timber.

'Did you see him?' he asked, still examining the door.

'Of course not, I wasn't here.'

'Did anyone see him?' he asked, looking over at me.

'See who?' I enquired, feeling I'd missed something.

'I can't have someone evicted on suspicion,' he exclaimed, shaking his head. 'If no one saw him, I can't do anything.'

'So that's it?' Fiona snapped, throwing her hands in the air. 'You're not going to do anything about this? How do you think Hettie's going to feel when she sees this? She'll be frightened out of her wits.'

'Well, I can get someone in to paint the door but not today.'

'Oh, go to hell,' she screamed. 'You're as bad as the pig that did this.' With that she entered the room, slamming the door in the manager's face. Fiona walked across the floor and sat on her bunk. 'We could stick something over it,' she said. 'A piece of paper or something.'

'Won't that look odd? Anyway, it's bound to fall off.'

'Suppose so,' Fiona nodded.

'We could scrape the door some more,' I suggested. 'You know, scratch off more paint so you can't see what it is. I've got a metal nail file.'

'Yes, I've got one too.'

'It's worth a try.'

For the next hour Fiona and I attacked the door with gusto, scratching and scraping away at the paintwork with our nail files. For the most part, the old paint was brittle, chipping away easily. However, towards the middle it was adhered to the timber like glue, requiring extra muscle. Admiring our handiwork, the door looked a mess with a large, perfectly square section of paint scraped away from the centre.

Brigit appeared just as we were finishing. She stared at the door, looked at the nail files in our hands, then stormed off downstairs obviously to report our vandalism to the manager. Ten minutes or so later, she returned alone, locking herself in the bathroom.

That evening as the others strolled in, no one commented on the door. To be perfectly honest, they didn't seem to have noticed it. After Angie's sedatives and my energetic bout of paint stripping, I was feeling tired. Having snacked on some fruit and yoghurt I decided on an early night, happy to leave the others to their own devices.

I called Michael first thing Monday morning, telling him I was still unwell and had best stay away. He seemed a little puzzled but accepted my story none the less. I felt cowardly, avoiding him like this. But I just needed to sort out my feelings before I entered into a confrontation. Besides, I wanted to be sure of the facts. At present, I only had a few superficial details to go on.

Hanging up the phone, I could smell the all-too-familiar aroma of burnt toast wafting from the dining room. The cook was obviously not thinking straight today with each piece charred and brittle. Choosing the least singed of the lot I joined Tom who was sitting alone, his brow creased, glancing at yesterday's paper.

'Sorted things out with Larry?' I asked, placing my toast and tea on the table.

'No, I bought a new model though,' Tom answered, folding his paper. 'This time I'll work solo.'

'Is everything all right?' I asked, noticing that Tom was not his jovial self. 'You still upset?'

'About Larry? No. My mother's place needs a bit of work. Wondering whether I shouldn't just sell the house and be done with it.'

'Will it cost a lot to fix?'

'Hard to say. I've been renting the place but even the tenants don't want it anymore. They're tired of the leaking roof leaving puddles. Said it's worse than having a dog that's not house trained.'

'Will it be hard to sell?'

'That's the problem. Cornwall's so far away. Outside of summer, there's not much of a demand for housing down there, especially in the state the place is in.'

'Can you get a loan?'

'Don't like my chances there,' he answered, taking a sip of his tea. 'Still, it'll work out, that's what my Mum would've said.'

I took my time strolling through Kensington Gardens, the thought of Fiona leaving was weighing on my mind. In the past months, she'd become more like a sister, or how I imagined a sister to be. Walking along the endless pathways, my feet buried in crinkled leaves, I felt overburdened with grief, mourning both the loss of a friendship, as well as the demise of a relationship.

At The Gazebo, I tried to conceal my reddened eyes by applying more mascara in the bathroom. Then when I felt I looked respectable, ventured into the kitchen.

As I entered the room Jane and Chef suddenly stopped speaking, a sure sign that they'd been talking about me. Smiling they said 'hello' in unison before introducing me to the new assistant, a lad in his teens who Chef had known in Camden. His name was Noah. Over a coffee I introduced myself to the young apprentice, making light conversation. Apart from the occasional muffled reply, Noah didn't say much.

'First day nerves,' I guessed, leaving the kitchen to ready the restaurant for the lunch diners.

'You didn't see Michael this weekend?' Jane asked, as we laid cloths over the tables.

'No, I wasn't well. Why?'

'Oh, we saw him on…over the weekend. Ran into him in Leicester Square.'

'Oh,' I said, suspecting Jane had also seen the mysterious blonde.

‘Everything all right?’ Jane enquired, after a pause. I looked at her questioningly. ‘You’re better now?’ she qualified.

‘Yes, I’m fine, just a 24-hour thing.’

The new assistant made Chef’s lot much easier. It was obvious the young lad held Chef in high esteem, eagerly carrying out every request with enthusiasm.

Ron kept to herself. Though I overheard her tell Gino that she’d met this “marvellously wealthy man”, at a party on Saturday night, and don’t be surprised if she runs off and elopes. Even though Gino laughed, I took her quite seriously and hoped it would come to pass. At least it would get her out of my face.

At closing, I deliberately ducked out before Jane and Chef offered me a lift home. I didn’t want to be subjected to an interrogation about Michael and I didn’t wish to feign ignorance either. As was increasingly becoming the case, I just wanted to be on my own.

25 September 1984

Male rats have been participating in homosexual behaviour. In colonies it is quite normal to see rats of the same gender hump each other and often it goes further than a fleeting attraction. Same-sex rats have often been observed in very affectionate, long-term relationships. As such, this is not seen as anything out of the ordinary.

The same cannot be said for the increase we are seeing in aggressive behaviour. Angst among the does has now reached the same proportion as buck incidents. Also, more buck/doe issues are emerging.

Chapter 21

The room was a hive of activity. Angie was busy selecting something to wear to court the next day. In one hand she was holding a black, long-sleeved, mini dress, in the other hand a studded, red, leather suit. Fiona suggested she wear trousers. But as Angie didn't have any, other than jeans, I offered to lend her a pair of mine, which she proceeded to try on for size.

Fiona had started to sort through her belongings, in preparation for her departure on Sunday. In her underwear drawer, she found a packet of stale cheese and a chocolate bar which had turned white.

Angie zipped up the trousers and looked in the mirror. They fitted her perfectly. After trying on one of my shirts, she decided to forgo her previous choices. In the midst of all this, Rick brought in a shoe box.

'New shoes?' Fiona remarked. 'You two are certainly going all out.'

'No, it was left outside the door,' he explained, passing it to Fi.

Gathering to view the box, we saw it had been tied with string, the words *Black Bitch* scribbled on the lid. Fiona pulled at the string and then resorted to scissors to break the tie, revealing the grisly contents inside. A black bird was lying dead in the box with a makeshift noose pulled tight around its neck, the word *Die* was scrawled in blood on the inside of the lid.

'Fuck he's sick. I'm taking this down to the manager.'

With exhibit number two in hand Fiona wasted no time in exiting the room, leaving Angie and Rick startled.

'What's that about?' Rick asked. 'Who's sick?'

'Oh, someone's got it in for Hettie,' I answered.

'Hettie?'

'Our new roommate,' Angie explained.

'Brigit's left?'

'No, they're boosting numbers here, remember. Each room is getting an extra tenant. I told you. Yours will be next. Honestly Rick, I'll be glad when this hearing's over. You don't listen to anything I say anymore.'

As expected, Fiona received little support from the manager who couldn't do anything unless he had proof.

'Maybe it's Brigit,' I said, noticing she was never around when these incidents occurred.

'No, Brigit's a nutter but she's not racist,' Fiona replied. 'At least I don't think she is.'

'Doing a bit of spring-cleaning Fi?' Rick commented, noticing Fiona sorting through her drawer.

'Oh, no, not really, I'm moving out.'

'What!' Angie exclaimed. 'You never told me, moving in with Julian?'

'No, going home actually.'

'You're going home. What back to your parents? Why?'

'Oh, a few problems at home,' she shrugged. 'Need to go back for a while.'

'So, when do you leave?'

'Sunday.'

'This Sunday, this week, why didn't you tell me?'

'It's all sort of happened so quickly,' Fiona explained. 'I was going to tell you, after the hearing, when things had quietened down.'

'We should go out, a farewell dinner,' Rick decided. 'How about Friday night?'

'I'm working,' I remarked, 'can't take the time off.'

'Saturday night then,' he suggested.

'No, not Saturday night. My train leaves early on Sunday,' Fiona replied. 'Don't want a late night.'

'Well, how about Saturday lunch?' Angie remarked.

'Yes, sounds good,' Fiona stated, while Rick and I nodded.

As they continued sorting through clothes and discussing the court proceedings, I quietly slipped into bed. Amidst the constant drone of conversation, I eventually closed my eyes, opening them to Angie's raucous laughter.

It was morning. Rick was standing in the room wearing a navy blue suit, white shirt and new tie. His shoes were polished to perfection, his hair gelled back. Angie was sending him up a little. But for all her smart remarks, she'd have to admit he looked very handsome. Rick was hurrying Angie along, as she fastened the last of her buttons. They had to be in court at nine and Rick was keen to get moving.

'Good luck,' we called as they left. Fiona crossed her fingers.

Waiting for me to get ready, Fiona chatted about her home. She seemed to be looking forward to the change in tempo and the security of family life. Sitting down to breakfast, she described the town where she grew up, the streets, the neighbours, the local landmarks and I envied her sense of belonging.

Ron was checking her watch as I strolled into The Gazebo. I was a few minutes late but I didn't bother apologising. Perhaps I'd adopted Fiona's devil-may-care attitude. After the anticipated verbal reprimand, I got on with my duties, hardly stopping until closing.

Leaving work, I noticed that Michael was out the front, sitting in his parked car. I wanted to get going, catch up with Rick and Angie. But I couldn't just keep walking.

'I've got to catch up with some friends tonight. Sorry, I should have called.'

Michael seemed peeved.

'What's going on?' he asked, somewhat abruptly.

'Another time, okay? I'm in a hurry.'

I could've asked Michael for a lift back to The Elms. But in all truth, I didn't feel like a showdown. At this point in time, I was more interested in the outcome of the hearing. Hurrying towards Kensington Gardens, I pondered the possible scenarios.

Opening the door to the room Angie looked devastated, sitting on her bunk, smoking a cigarette.

'It didn't go well?' I asked.

Fiona looked up from her magazine as Angie shook her head.

'It did go well,' Fiona gloated. 'Just that miss here doesn't like it.'

'Rick got visitation rights?' I asked.

'Yes, three hours every second Saturday,' Fiona replied. 'Angie's put out.'

'Oh, shut up,' Angie snapped. 'It's got nothing to do with you.'

'But it's true, isn't it? You wanted him to lose. You were praying he'd never see his kids again.'

'I said shut up.'

'Why because you're a right selfish bitch. If you ask me, he's too good for you.'

'If you don't shut up, I'll…'

'Okay, okay,' I said, 'enough, eh?'

'It's not that I didn't want Rick to see his kids,' Angie sniffed, 'I didn't want him to see her. The visitation rights have these conditions attached. He must collect the boys from the family home and return them three hours later. He can't take them more than five kilometres. It just means that they'll be thrown together every second weekend. That's why I'm put out, not because of what fat arse says.'

'Oh, and who's calling me a fat arse, better than yours.'

'Give it a rest,' I interrupted. 'You two are becoming unbearable. You're always at each other.' Escaping to the bathroom, I threw cold water onto my face before re-emerging refreshed and prepared for round two. 'Where's Rick?' I asked.

'He's out with Peter celebrating,' Fiona smiled, happy to have something to rub into Angie's face.

'And Hettie?'

'She's gone to the opera. The things she crams into a day,' Fiona remarked. 'I reckon she's seen more of London than I have.'

'No more trouble?' I asked.

'No, the manager said he had a word with Timothy who denied it all, of course. Still, it may have put the wind up him. Nothing's happened today.'

Rick didn't return to the room and Angie was still sulking in the morning. Fiona was waiting for any opportunity to pounce, but I managed to keep her quiet. Hettie had come back during the night and was gone again by the time I awoke. Lying in bed, willing myself to get up, I wished her energy was contagious.

First thing at work, Gino handed each of us a pile of questionnaires for our customers.

'When do we hand them out?' Jane asked.

'With the bill, there's a complimentary pen that goes with each one.'

At closing, Gino rounded up the responses. Jane had collected 19 and I had 22. When asked for her contribution, Ron simply said that no one was interested in filling them out. Customers had better things to do with their time.

Ron's lack of co-operation continued for the rest of the working week. Even so, come Friday night, Gino had a box full of completed questionnaires.

‘It’s because she’s such a bad waitress,’ Jane remarked, as Chef drove me home. ‘That’s why she won’t hand out the questionnaires.’

‘Yes,’ I agreed. ‘I think it’s her appalling service that has caused the downturn in business. If Gino doesn’t realise that soon, there won’t be any customers to fill in surveys.’

Fiona was packing as I walked into the room. On seeing me, she threw me an envelope. I recognised the scrawled handwriting and the red ink. Inside was a message made up with cut out letters:

Rid London of the Black Plague.

‘Are you going to show this to the manager?’ I asked.

‘What’s the point? He won’t do anything unless he has proof. I’m only glad she’s leaving tomorrow. Otherwise, this nutter could do something stupid.’

‘You haven’t shown Hettie then?’

‘No,’ Fiona answered, folding her work skirts and placing them into the case. ‘It’s embarrassing. As though we all think like him.’

Come morning Hettie was up early, her backpack crammed full and secured for the flight back to Guyana. After we’d waved her off, Fiona took a deep breath.

‘Well now you can rest easy,’ she said, looking at me. ‘You already have one nutter to deal with, you don’t need some other maniac stalking the room.’

I nodded.

Looking across at the all-familiar sight of Fiona sitting on her bed, I realised how much I was going to miss her company. Still there was time for sadness tomorrow, today was for celebrating.

Fiona had suggested having her farewell lunch at one of the open-air restaurants in Covent Garden. It was a sunny morning, so we all nodded in agreement. Next Fiona suggested we walk there instead of taking public transport. We all shook our heads and Fiona was outnumbered three to one.

Walking down to the tube we chatted, in high spirits, a burst of sunshine taking the bite off an otherwise chilly, autumn day. Rick’s smile never left his face as he playfully kissed Angie’s cheek and held Fiona’s hand affectionately. The tube trip came to pass without any of us realising we’d been travelling. Instead, we listened to a blow-by-blow account of the hearing.

Arriving at Convent Garden we secured a table, not that there was any rush to do so. As popular as the area was with tourists, today it was quiet, most considering it too cold to eat outside. As the sun streamed down upon us, Rick positioned the umbrella. For hours we drank and ate, enjoying each other's company, knowing it was the last time we'd all be together.

'Here's to Fi,' Rick toasted, standing with a glass of beer in hand. 'May she come back soon.'

'Hear, hear,' we all said, downing our drinks.

'And here's to Rick, Eddy and Max,' Fiona responded. 'May you make up for lost time and more.'

'Thanks,' Rick said and again we all drank.

'And here's to Angie,' Rick added. 'May she say yes to my proposal of marriage.'

At this we all went quiet.

'What proposal of marriage?' Angie asked, bewildered.

'The one you just heard,' Rick answered.

'Jesus Rick, no one can call you a romantic,' Fiona laughed.

'Is that how you're going to propose? Like that?' Angie enquired, light-heartedly.

Rick looked around at our scrutinising eyes.

'Okay,' he said, then taking Angie's hand. 'Angie, will you do me the honour of being my wife.' We all smiled and then Rick continued: 'Because if you don't say yes now, I may never get drunk enough to propose to you in the future.'

Amidst our laughter, Angie nodded her head in acceptance. As they kissed, I noticed Fiona was looking over at the next table. Sitting there was a blonde woman with her back to us. Fiona nudged me and pointed.

'That's her,' she said.

'Who?' I asked.

'The one that was on with Michael. You know, sticking her tongue down his throat and playing with him under the table.'

I looked at the woman closely. From the back, I was sure it wasn't Tanya, much too short for one thing and a very different hairstyle. Perhaps Fiona had been wrong. Maybe it hadn't been Michael and here I was ignoring him for no reason.

While we continued toasting anything and everything, I kept an eye on the woman. I was hoping to catch a glimpse as soon as she turned around. One hour passed and then two, yet the woman remained facing away from me looking at her female companion.

‘How’d you know it was her? You can hardly see her,’ I remarked, while Rick and Angie were chatting.

‘I saw her walk over to the table. It’s her all right.’

As Rick ordered some more drinks the stranger pulled out her wallet, placed money on the table, then stood and turned around. Suddenly her eyes caught mine and she smiled, coming over to give me one of those kisses that never quite touches your cheek.

‘Elizabeth,’ she called. ‘Haven’t seen you for ages.’ Fiona raised her eyebrows.

‘You’ve dyed your hair,’ I said. ‘It used to be red.’

‘Yes, do you like it? Anyway, blondes have more fun, so they say.’

‘Well, you certainly do,’ Fiona sniped.

‘Oh, Fiona, Angie and Rick,’ I said, ‘this is Penny. Michael’s stylist.’

Angie and Rick nodded and smiled, while I seethed inside. I wanted to confront her, instead I managed to keep my cool. As she ranted and raved about something or other they were working on, I was remembering all those incidents I’d overlooked. Her contempt for Tanya, the lace lingerie she left at Michael’s place, even the shirt she’d given me. How did she come to be so near to The Elms first thing in the morning? Obviously, she’d been with Michael. When she eventually left, I was shaking with rage.

‘You should’ve hit her,’ Fiona said. ‘Do you want me to?’

‘No, it’s fine.’

‘Why do you want to hit her? She seemed nice enough to me,’ Angie said.

‘She’s bonking Michael,’ Fiona explained.

‘No, really?’

The stony look on my face put an end to the conversation, the jovial atmosphere now stifled by the subdued undertone.

It was early evening by the time we dragged our intoxicated bodies back home. With a few drinks under your belt, The Elms appeared almost stately until you looked closely, then you saw its ugly side.

‘Do you mind,’ Brigit snarled. ‘I’m trying to get some sleep.’

‘Lighten up Brigit, it’s Fiona’s last night,’ Angie exclaimed.

‘Good, no more stinking sanitary pads in the bathroom,’ she smirked.

‘You use sanitary pads,’ Angie giggled, then suddenly, ‘oh,’ as she realised the reason why.

'God, you're a fucking bitch. You're a right smart-mouthed witch,' Fiona screamed, lunging at Brigit. Angie and I pulled her back. 'No, let me fucking whack her in her fucking evil mouth. I've wanted to for months. Let me, just this once, wipe that fucking sneer of her fucking ugly, twisted, bitter…'

We managed to contain Fiona's fist. Though I don't know why we just didn't let Fi punch her. Truth was we all wanted to smack Brigit. This was as good a time as any. However common sense prevailed and, with Fiona now settled on her bunk, the heat of the moment had passed. If anything was to put a damper on our high spirits that did. Angie, sat quietly, probably musing over her comments about Julian. She now knew why Fiona was leaving and she'd been hit with a case of the guilts. Rick had climbed onto the top bunk and dropped off to sleep, snoring profusely. Brigit remained in bed, reading that same Home Hints magazine. While I disappeared into the bathroom, sitting on the floor, thinking about Penny.

As I emerged, refreshed from a quick dunking in the basin, I noticed Brigit was asleep, her magazine sprawled open on the floor. She'd been reading about *Acquiring the Cottage Touch*, *The Safe Storage of Flammable Liquids* and *How to Dry Clean Clothes like the Professionals*.

With everyone else in bed, I followed suit and before too long it seemed Fiona was waking me.

'How about breakfast for old times?' she asked. 'See you downstairs in half an hour.'

In the dining room, Fiona had secured a corner table, a little sweaty from her walk through the gardens, she was digging into a healthy helping of toast washed down with tea.

'Sad?' I asked, joining her at the table.

'You kidding? They make the worst toast here. Only eat the stuff because it's free.' She looked at me, a hint of tears in her eyes. 'Yes, a little,' she acknowledged. 'I'll miss some things.'

'Like what?' I asked, jokingly.

'Like Angie's and Rick's fights. How many times did we have to wait for the bathroom because they were screaming and yelling in there? I'll miss that. Strange, eh? Still, I don't reckon their marriage will be bliss. Imagine living next door to them, you'd never get any peace.' Fiona took another bite of her toast as we pondered the last few months. 'Remember the bus trip, all those girls with the bags? I mean we may as well have had signs around our necks. And those two old biddies, they weren't too pleased,' she laughed. 'And how about the rotten meat? You weren't half sick, were you? And Brigit clawing you around the neck? Honestly you should have let me hit her, she had it coming.' I nodded. 'Yes, I won't forget this place in a hurry. Don't think any of us will.'

'Can I come to the station?' I asked.

'To see me off?' I nodded. 'Sure can,' Fiona replied. 'I was hoping you would.'

Upstairs Fiona slowly checked the room then, grabbing her case, stopped at the door for one final glance.

The tube trip to St Pancras was quiet, neither of us wishing to speak. Arriving at the busy British Rail Station, Fiona led me to the appropriate platform where we made small talk until it was time to board.

As the whistle sounded and the train edged forward, I followed the carriage waving until it was out of view. I stood momentarily and stared ahead, then dropped to my knees and cried. I sobbed like a child, without control nor care for what others may think. My ribs hurt from the heaving motion and my stomach ached. Yet the tears kept coming in waves. Londoners, being Londoners, walked past my crumpled frame, casually turning away. Eventually gaining some self-control, I stood and wiped my eyes before taking the tube train home.

30 September 1984

Given the increase in population there are now too many adverse episodes to document so the opposite will now be applied. Going forward only positive interactions will be recorded.

On that note, however, there have not been too many pleasantries to report. Even amicable encounters have all somehow ended with some display of anxiety, act of violence or even a degree of depression. This new method of reporting has been added as a protocol amendment.

Chapter 22

Sitting on my bunk, I looked around at the empty room. I noticed Fiona had even taken her dead plant. Before too long Angie and Rick would be married and moving as well, leaving me with Brigit. It was a depressing thought.

After splashing my face with some water, I looked at my reflection in the bathroom mirror. It was a haunting reminder of the first day I'd arrived at The Elms, drawn and pallid from jet lag. It seemed so much had changed, yet so little.

Brigit was now back in the room; I could hear the floor creaking. If it was Angie she would have spoken, asked me about Fiona's farewell at the station. But not Brigit. No, I'd come to the conclusion long ago that Brigit's behaviour defied all reason.

Walking into the room, refreshed from the cool water, I noticed Brigit was standing by the window. She suddenly jammed something into her pocket, turned, picked up her bag and hastily left the room. I wandered over to the window sill, saw Angie's cigarettes and her pills, as well as her odd assortment of beauty aids.

'What could have possibly taken her interest?' I thought.

The room was cold. It was only the start of autumn but there was a definite chill in the air. I imagined that before too long I'd be waking up with ice over my covers. The heating didn't seem to work here but, then again, neither did the air conditioning. The damp, cool air was making me drowsy and I thought I could probably do with a nap.

Fully clothed I hopped under the duvet. I could hear the muffled voices of the neighbouring residents but, after a while, the door banged shut and the room fell silent. So, listening to the traffic outside, I allowed its monotonous hum to lull me to sleep.

I don't know how long I dozed but my coughing woke me. I could smell bread being toasted in the kitchen. I coughed again. Opening my eyes, the room seemed dark, much darker than I expected.

'Must have overslept,' I thought, before realising it was smoke that had robbed the room of its light.

Coughing I jumped out of bed and rushed to the door. The doorknob singed my hand as I attempted to turn it. After grabbing a towel, I tried again. Even through the material, the metal handle was burning hot and smoke was pouring in through the gap under the door. Hurrying into the bathroom, I wet the towel and tried the handle again. The door was locked. It wouldn't open. Quickly I stuffed the wet towel under the door, thinking it might stop the flames burning their way through.

In the hazy, smoke-filled room, I searched for my keys. I was sure I'd left them on the chest of drawers, or maybe in my bag. Perhaps they were in the bathroom. The room was blackening by the second retarding my vision considerably. Coughing, I shielded my face with the bottom of my sweater. I could hear the door burning, roaring like a bonfire. It was only a matter of minutes before the flames would engulf the room. With no other way out, I looked for something to break the window pane.

After pulling out a drawer and turning it upside down to empty it of contents, I grabbed the cumbersome piece of wood. Covering my face with a quilt I took aim at the window, striking at it with all my might. I could hear the sound of breaking glass, followed by a whiff of fresh air. Yet, for all my effort, only a tiny piece of the window had been broken. The room was now so blackened I could hardly breathe.

Sticking my head through the small gap in the window, I took a deep gasp. Then, with drawer in hand, I had yet another go at the glass. This time I shattered a large section, busily chipping away at the rest until most of the glass had been removed. Tears were streaming down my face and I was coughing constantly now, the air from the window providing some welcome relief. Looking out, I saw Busman staring up at me angrily.

'Fire,' I yelled. 'There's a fire up here.'

Outside the window there was a small, narrow ledge. I wondered if I could walk along it to the next room, although I didn't like my chances. Suddenly there was a small explosion as pieces of the door flew into the room, the flames reaching inside as if looking for something to grasp. With no other option I stepped out onto the ledge, determined not to look down at the pavement far below. The ledge was wide enough to give me a foothold, as I clawed at pieces of plaster work jutting out from the facade. In places the exterior was chipped through to the brickwork, providing small gaps in which to secure my fingers. Edging my way along, I could hear a mumble of voices below. Obviously, a crowd of onlookers had gathered, but I didn't dare look down.

The first window I came to was shut, so I continued on my way. The second window seemed to be shut, but thankfully the far side was opened enough for me to slip through.

Pushing one leg in the opened window, I found a chair and then pulled the rest of my body inside. Suddenly I saw Larry, cowering in the corner of his bunk. The ship model clutched in his hands. By the look on his face, he seemed to think I was after his galleon.

'There's a fire Larry, we've got to get out. Where are the emergency stairs?' Larry stared at me in fear, still gripping the model tightly in his arms. 'Listen Larry, there's a fire. We've got to get out.'

Reaching over to grab Larry, he shrunk away from my arms. He was squeezing the model so tightly I thought it would snap in his hold. Grabbing at him again I managed to grip his shirt then, pulling with all my might, got him up on his feet. Larry was trying to push me away, hitting out at me with his fist. But as he wouldn't let go of his treasure, his force was impeded somewhat. Pulling him towards the door, I managed to turn the handle. A mass of flames covered one end of the corridor, preventing us from taking the stairs.

The smoke was so strong it took my breath away, while the heat stung my skin like acid. Larry started to cry, nursing his model like a baby. Pulling him onto his knees, I told him to crawl.

'Where's the emergency exit?' I yelled, as we eased our way along.

My eyes were stinging and I was gasping for breath. Larry didn't reply and instead sobbed like a child.

Crawling the length of the corridor, we found the emergency sign. Jumping up to open the door, I screamed in frustration and anger. The door was locked and the key had been removed. I kicked the door with my foot and swore. Larry cowered in the corner as if expecting to be hit, his body shaking from my outburst.

'It's locked, Larry, the door's locked. Is there another one?' I asked, shaking his arm for some response. Larry seemed terrified of me, pulling his body up into the foetal position and sinking further into the wall. 'It's okay, Larry. I'm trying to get us out. Is there another exit? Another way we can get out?' Larry just trembled, his body recoiling.

Grabbing him by the arm we proceeded to crawl back into the hallway, the window in one of the rooms seemed the only way out. As we turned the corner the heat burnt my eyes, the flames were now much closer.

The roar of the fire was almost deafening, interspersed with crackling, crashing sounds as large sections of the wall began to collapse. Amidst the racket, I could hear the faint sound of a siren and, endeavouring to get to a window, dragged Larry along.

Every room we came to was locked and the fire was fast approaching. It was no use going any further, so I turned and led Larry back to the emergency door. Larry's model was now too hot to hold and he dropped it on the floor.

'We'll wait here,' I gasped, propping Larry against the wall. 'The firemen are here. They'll get us out.'

The air was now black with smoke, wafting around the corner. My eyes were watering and I could taste the soot in my mouth. My lips were burnt as was the hair in my nostrils. Breathing was becoming increasingly difficult, coughing with every inhale. My skin was soaked in perspiration; a slimy, greasy residue that seemed to fry in the heat. Larry was having trouble breathing, his gasps becoming slower by the second. I wiped his face, his body moisture wetting my hand.

'Won't be long now Larry. Hang in there,' I said, exhausted.

I closed my eyes and sat back to conserve my energy. After a few minutes, I could hear noise from the stairwell, the sound of heavy boots and shouting followed by banging. It seemed to be coming nearer.

'They're on the floor below,' I told Larry, his eyes shut to repel the acidic air. The noise was clearer now, it was the firemen. 'We're here,' I shouted, collapsing in a coughing heap. 'We're here,' I yelled again, banging my fist against the door and burning it in the process.

'Move back,' I heard, from the other side of the door, so holding Larry by the arm, we edged our way to the opposite wall.

One hit, two hits, three hits, four, until the silver blade of an axe could be seen breaking through the timber. As pieces of wood splintered and fell to the floor, there stood two firemen in gas masks and protective clothes. On seeing the alien sight before him, Larry panicked. Falling onto the floor, he backed away from the firemen terrified.

'Larry, come back. It's only the firemen,' I called, but he was already around the corner.

Pushing me into the stairwell, one of the firemen followed Larry who was now shouting at him to stay away. A few seconds later, I heard a kerfuffle, followed by an agonising scream. Breaking free from my attendant, I ran back into the corridor just as Larry's body ignited into a mass of flames. That's the last I remember, everything blacking out around me. Even Larry's screams suddenly extinguished.

When I eventually came to, a watch was dangling in front of my eyes. I saw a woman in a white dress leaning over me and then I saw no more.

For the next few days, I came in and out of consciousness. My only recollection was an incredible thirst that never subsided, leaving my lips dry and my throat red raw.

When I awoke today, I saw Tom staring at me.

'Well, hello there sleeping beauty,' he grinned.

'How long have you been here?' I whispered, my throat burning with each word.

'Since Sunday,' he replied, moving his chair closer.

'What day is it?'

'Thursday.'

I shut my eyes again, everything was still hazy. I couldn't have been here that long.

'There was a fire,' I explained.

'Yes, that there was.'

'You made it okay,' I said.

'And I'm pleased to say that you did too.'

'Larry?' I asked. Tom paused and then softly shook his head. 'Oh,' I mumbled, my eyes stinging with tears.

'Now don't you go getting all upset. They'll send me off they will. You did your best, Elizabeth. Anyway, they said it was quick,' Tom remarked, wiping my eyes with a tissue. 'It would have been worse if he'd survived.'

When Tom had moved away, I noticed my hands were bound in bandages.

'My hands?' I asked.

'Burnt, but they'll mend. They reckon there's been no permanent damage. More smoke inhalation than anything. They cut your hair. They had to. It was burnt 'round the ends.'

I looked to see but my hair was in a cap.

As I licked my dry lips, Tom reached for the glass of water on my bedside table. After leaning forward to take a sip, I was thoroughly worn out. Lying back on the pillow, I drifted off to sleep.

Friday, I awoke again. Tom was sitting in the chair, reading a newspaper.

'What time is it?' I asked.

'Just after three in the afternoon. How are you?'

'Thirsty,' I replied, trying to reach the glass with my heavily bandaged hands.

'I'll help you,' offered Tom, holding me up to take a few sips.

'Anything about the fire?' I asked, nodding to the paper.

'Yes, they've been cleaning up the mess. Surprised there weren't more fatalities.'

'How many were there?'

'Two. Larry and that lass who shared your room.'

'Angie?' I asked, suddenly panicked.

'No, that's not her name.'

'Brigit?'

'Yes, that's the one.'

Saturday, I managed to eat my first meal since the fire; custard and pears. The inside of my mouth was tender, probably burnt from the heat, so I took each spoonful slowly, washing it down with water I sipped through a straw.

The bandages reminded me of boxing gloves. You couldn't find your fingers in them. Still Tom assured me they'd be coming off next week. Any sooner and my burns could become infected.

Sunday, flowers arrived from Michael. Tom said that Michael had sent four dozen roses on Monday but they'd died by the time I came 'round. He also said that he'd seen Michael enquiring about me at the desk. But they wouldn't let Michael in because I wasn't allowed to have visitors.

'How'd you get in?' I asked.

'I told them I was your brother.'

By Monday, I was enjoying three mushy meals a day. I had mastered the bandages enough to hold a spoon and direct it into my mouth. When they removed the cap, I saw my hair was now shoulder-length and I was grateful there weren't great bald patches spread over my scalp. Angie and Rick called in on Monday night, just as Tom was leaving.

'God you were lucky,' Angie said, giving me a kiss.

'Yes, lady luck was on your side, all right,' Rick added.

'How long will you be in here?' Angie asked. 'Not a bad room. Great view.'

'I don't know. Until they take the bandages off, I suppose.'

'What did you have for dinner?' Rick asked, trying to guess by the remains in my bowl.

'Custard and fruit salad,' I answered.

'Is that all?' he enquired. 'Don't think much of the meals.'

'Well, it was Brigit,' Angie remarked, taking a seat.

'What was?' I asked, trying to mentally adjust to the change in conversation.

'Brigit lit the fire,' she explained.

'How do you know?'

'It was in the paper. Apparently, she poured this flammable liquid all around our door and along the carpet to the stairs, then set it alight. They think she caught fire trying to get away. They found her body in the emergency stairwell.'

'Oh,' I commented, not really knowing what else to say.

'Well, like the witch that she was, she got burnt at the stake,' Angie added. Rick and I just stared open-mouthed. 'Well don't look at me like that,' she stated. 'She deserved it. Just about killed you and what about poor, old Larry?'

'So, how are you feeling?' Rick asked, sitting on the bed. 'They wouldn't let us in before today. We figured you must be in a bad way.'

'Oh, I'm fine, getting stronger every day.'

'Listen we were going to call Fi. Let her know the news. She's probably seen it in the paper. But I didn't know her last name.'

'Rolland,' I answered.

'Fiona Rolland,' Angie repeated, and then laughed. 'Funny, eh? We all lived in each other's pockets yet we'd never been formerly introduced.'

'Did they find you another room at The Elms?' I asked.

'You're joking? The place has been gutted,' Rick said. 'Two floors completely burnt out and the rest damaged by smoke and water. No, everyone's been relocated.'

'They found us a room of our own in Bayswater,' Angie added. 'It suits us perfectly. We even have our own bathroom.'

'So, have all our things been destroyed?' I asked.

'Everything,' Angie answered. 'But don't you go worrying. We're going to have them replaced, as soon as the insurance comes through.'

Tuesday, as I washed, a nurse came in to say that Michael wished to see me. I told her I didn't want any visitors and she kindly passed on the message. Later that day flowers arrived from Jane, Chef and Gino saying they were sorry they couldn't get away from work, but they'd be in to see me soon. The flowers were promptly placed in a vase alongside the bunch from Michael, the ones from Angie and Rick, as well as the carnations from David Hetherington, manager of The Elms. Strange, I never thought of him as having a name before now.

Wednesday evening, Busman came in with Tom. They'd been relocated to a hotel in Earl's Court. It had upset Busman's schedules a little, but he was working around it. I told them the doctor would be removing my bandages tomorrow and Tom promised to call in.

As expected, the doctor arrived just after lunch on Thursday. Even though he'd warned me that my hands might look ghastly, in time he assured me they'd heal. As he unfolded the bandages, I waited in anticipation. A seemingly endless length of bandage was removed and handed over to the nurse for disposal, then another length and another until I wondered if my hands were in there at all.

Finally, he came to a layer of gauze and, removing it with tweezers, revealed the hideously askew skin underneath. Turning over my hands by the fingertips, he inspected the palms where most of the damage had occurred, obviously from gripping the door handles. The skin was unrecognisable as such and instead looked like two pieces of contaminated, raw steak.

'We'll wrap these hands in lighter bandages this time. That way you'll have more movement. Coming along well,' he added.

When Tom arrived, I was depressed and crying, probably an after effect of the whole ordeal.

'There there, it will get better, you'll see. You're over the worst of it now.'

'You haven't seen my hands.'

'I know they look bad, but the doctor said there'll be no permanent damage. It just takes time that's all. What you need is some clean, sea air. It's a tonic if ever there was one.'

'What are you talking about?' I snapped. 'I've got no clothes, nowhere to live, I can't even go back to work because I can't use these hands and you think all it's going to take is a stroll along Brighton Beach.'

'Not Brighton. I was thinking of Cornwall. My mother's place.' I stared at him blankly. 'You know how I was saying that my mother's house needed work?' I nodded. 'Well, the tenants have moved out. I'm not too keen on this place in Earl's Court so I was thinking of going back to Cornwall, doing the maintenance work myself and then eventually coming back here to London. It'll take about six months, by my estimations. So, I was wondering if you'd like to come along. There are two bedrooms, you'd have your privacy. Just the place to get your health back. Mind you,' he continued, 'it's nothing flash, just a cottage. The garden's overgrown and the thatched roof's leaking as well you know. But it's serene and homely. So, you give it some thought and let me know what you think. There's no rush,' he added, patting my arm.

Tom stayed for an hour or so, chatting about the new refurbishment they're planning for The Elms, then called it a night. Long after he'd gone, I was still awake considering life in Cornwall.

Friday, they changed my dressing and I was pleased to see there was a small sign of improvement. Also, I noticed my appetite had returned, eating three decent sized meals as well as morning and afternoon tea. When Tom turned up in the evening, I told him my decision. I would like to go to Cornwall, if he hadn't changed his mind.

'I think that's wise, Elizabeth. Give you time to get well. Recover fully. London's not going anywhere. It'll still be here when you get back.'

I smiled.

'Anyway, I've always wanted to live in a cottage, especially one with a thatched roof,' I said.

'Well don't you go thinking it's anything special. Once you've lived with a leaking thatched roof, you'd give anything to have slate,' he stated. 'That Michael was in here before. Not that it's any of my business but you really ought to talk to him, sort out whatever's gone wrong.'

'How do you know so much about Michael?' I asked.

'I've got eyes, I've seen him picking you up and dropping you off. He seems nice enough.' I nodded, tears coming to my eyes. 'Now there's nothing to be sad about. The sea air and salt water await. You'll like Cornwall Elizabeth.'

Jane and Chef called in on Saturday.

'I can give you some clothes,' Jane offered. 'I've put on over five kilos, outgrown heaps of things. Good clothes too. I think you'll like them.'

I needed clothes desperately. All my things had been destroyed in the fire. I thanked Jane for her offer.

Angie called in later and I asked her to purchase some bras and knickers for me, giving her money that Tom had left in the top drawer. She said she'd be happy to buy whatever I wanted. After making a list, I felt more optimistic about the future. At least I wouldn't have to travel down to Cornwall in my backless, hospital gown.

Sunday, Jane dropped off a suitcase filled with jeans, trousers, skirts, shirts, a veritable wardrobe of clothes. She'd also bought me a new pair of shoes, knowing we took the same size. I thanked her profusely, offering to pay her something. However, she refused.

'I'm never going to fit into them again, not with Albert's cooking. Besides we need the room in the wardrobe. We've been really short of storage space since we moved in together.'

Come morning, Angie was my first visitor with all the personal items I'd requested. She told me she couldn't locate Fiona. There seemed to be hundreds of Rollands up north and Angie couldn't afford that many long-distance calls. Deep down, I was pleased that Fiona couldn't be located. At this point in time, she had enough problems of her own.

I was now ready to leave the hospital. Unfortunately, the doctor didn't agree, saying I'd be in hospital for another three days at least with regular check-ups for some time after that. When I told him I'd be in Cornwall, he offered to refer me to a doctor in Truro. The thought of ongoing medical treatment left me feeling low. Still, I had to follow doctor's orders if my hands were to fully heal.

Wednesday, Larry was buried. I didn't go to the funeral but a few from The Elms paid their last respects, along with Larry's sister and her family. Tom and Busman said it was a simple service, just what Larry would've wanted.

'After all,' Busman added, 'Larry never did like crowds.'

Come Thursday, the doctor changed my bandages and informed me I'd be discharged tomorrow. When I told Tom he said he'd arrange our train tickets immediately, so we could leave London just after midday.

As soon as the morning sun shone through the window, I was up and about, busily preparing to leave. My attitude was a sure sign that I was feeling better.

After the doctor checked my wounds, he handed me a referral. With discharge papers in hand, I was escorted downstairs by the ward sister.

There was a cab waiting outside which took us to the bank, in order to withdraw my savings, and then onto Michael's house. We arrived at the mews mid-morning. I was hoping he'd still be home.

As I walked up the alley, I looked down at what I was wearing; a black tailored jacket, almost as long as the mini skirt it covered, a black top, stockings and shoes. I was wearing a black beret, as well as black woollen gloves to conceal my still bandaged hands. By the heavy use of black, I could have been going to a funeral. Perhaps I was.

Knocking on the front door, I heard movement on the first floor. Michael was still in bed. By the thumping noise that followed, Michael was descending the stairs. Looking up I noticed the drapes at his window move. Obviously, he wasn't alone. Opening the door, he seemed surprised to see me.

'I just came to say good-bye. I'm leaving London.'

Michael seemed stunned by my news and brushed his hair back with his hand.

'When?'

'Today. Just after one.'

Michael looked at his watch.

'Don't you think it's a bit sudden?' he asked, stroking his chin with his hand.

'No, it's long overdue.'

'Well, can I drive you to the airport? I'll only take a second to get dressed.'

'No, I have a cab waiting.'

'Well would you like to come in for a minute?'

'No,' I shook my head. 'I don't think Penny would like it.' Michael looked upwards and then took a deep breath.

'You know, it's not what you think, it's just…' Suddenly I placed my finger on Michael's lips.

'Ssh,' I said, quietly. 'Don't add insult to injury.'

As he took in the meaning of my words, his eyes glistened with tears. Touching my outstretched hand gently, he kissed my gloved fingers before placing his arms around me and holding me tightly. Michael started to sob, his chest heaving with each gasp. I remained detached, unsure of how or what I felt. After a few minutes, I said that I had to go and Michael released his grip. I looked at him one more time. His tall frame seemed somewhat shorter. The lines around his red eyes robbed him of his youthful looks. Stroking the stubble on his cheek, I turned and walked away.

My companion for the next six months was waiting by the cab door. After helping me in, he told the driver our destination. As we weaved our way through the London Streets, I mentally farewelled the bag ladies who stood on the corners, never moving with the lights. I noted the striking miners, shaking collection tins at every tube station. I waved good-bye to the parks, home to countless down-and-outs. Then I looked over at my adopted big brother and thought of the cottage awaiting us in Cornwall.

'Not long now,' he said, pointing to the British Rail station up ahead. I smiled at Tom and nodded.

Obituary

Lawrence Theodore Standish MSc MRes DClinPsy Camb
4 January 1926–30 September 1984

The death of Professor Lawrence Standish has shocked the scientific community, not only in the UK but throughout the world.

Educated at Eton College, the University of Cambridge and Harvard, Standish had degrees in science and research with a doctorate in clinical psychology, a passion his family believes was fuelled by his own mental health issues.

For more than two decades, Standish was a prolific contributor to the *British Journal of Medical Science*. His many papers credited with challenging the perceptions of mental health, especially among those working in medical fields. Many also cite Standish when discussing the modifications to treatments over the years, particularly with regard to drug therapies.

Standish was a regular keynote speaker at scientific symposiums, here in the UK and at academic institutions internationally. Though, in recent years, his ailing health prevented him appearing at these forums.

In 1979 Standish, having experienced episodes of paranoia and hallucinations, was diagnosed with schizophrenia. Subsequently, his research suffered when funding was stopped, after it was discovered that Standish was sabotaging his own project.

Undeterred, Standish continued with his life's work after selling his South Kensington townhouse to finance his experiments. In fact, he was researching the impact of population on behaviour at the time of his death.

Standish died in a fire at a London hotel where he had been living.

He is survived by his sister, Hillary.